MIST *on the* MOORS

Elizabeth Penney

Annie's®
AnniesFiction.com

Books in the Secrets of the Quilt series

Library of Congress-in-Publication Data
Mist on the Moors / by Elizabeth Penney
p. cm.
I. Title
                    2016936757

AnniesFiction.com
(800) 282-6643
Secrets of the Quilt™
Series Creator: Shari Lohner
Series Editors: Shari Lohner, Janice Tate, and Ken Tate
Cover Illustrator: Jonathan Bouw

10 11 12 13 14 | Printed in China | 9 8 7 6 5 4 3 2

1

Cabot Falls, Vermont,
Present Day

Sofia Parker pulled up the bedspread and gave the pillows a final fluff, then glanced at her bedside clock. Only one o'clock. The day was dragging, thanks to a bad case of the jitters. At four, she was meeting with a wealthy client out on Lake Lucy, and this would be her biggest catering job yet. She'd worked on the menus for days.

What on earth should I do until then? She was too restless to read a novel, and the daily housework was now complete. Her glance fell on the Renaissance-era *cassone* standing in a corner.

Do I have time? Well, maybe for a peek. Sofia lifted the lid of the carved wooden trunk, which held the antique quilt she'd inherited from her dear Italian grandmother, Elena Baresi. The quilt consisted of squares cut from historic fabrics, and as Sofia pulled back the plain muslin cloth covering it, the muted reds and blues and greens glimmered. The fabrics were faded, yes, but thanks to her ancestors' care, they were in remarkably good shape.

Due to its fragility, she didn't take the quilt out of the trunk often. So today she tucked the treasure in again, like a precious baby, and pulled out the leather diary instead. Compiled in the early 1900s when the quilt had been sewn together, the diary had an entry corresponding to each square. After carefully closing the trunk's lid, she carried the book to the green-and-ivory striped armchair, her favorite reading spot.

Where are you taking me this time, Nonna? Sofia and her fellow Pinot Painters, Julie Butler and Marla Dixon, were investigating the history behind each square. So far, the stories they'd discovered had been fascinating, offering glimpses into another time and place. Each ancestor had faced difficulties that taxed their creativity and required the use of their individual gifts. Sofia wondered if that was why Nonna left the quilt to her instead of her sisters. She often found her own creativity stretched with the challenge of raising four children while trying to establish an artisan-quality catering business.

She caught her breath at the thought of the meeting later that afternoon. Prominent citizens from all over Vermont would be attending the charity auction she was catering. It was a huge step for her fledgling business.

Forcing herself to settle down, Sofia gently leafed to the next entry, the eighth one. *Beatrice Alice Kimble, The Yorkshire Moors, England, 1850.* Another ancestor in England. Initially she had expected all the entries to feature women who lived in Italy. She read on. *Aha!* Apparently Beatrice Kimble had worked for the National Gallery, and her specialty had been Italian Renaissance art. There was a link back to Italy.

Absorbed, Sofia continued to read, translating the entry as she went and making notes. Beatrice's square was cut from something called a *scialle di merletto*—a black lace shawl. She remembered the piece well since it wasn't a solid fabric, although it was backed by white cotton. The elaborate design of flowers and leaves was as delicate as a pen-and-ink drawing.

"Hey, Mom, are we still going out to see Mrs. Stanley?"

Sofia jumped. She looked up to see her older daughter, Vanessa, standing in the bedroom doorway.

Sofia put one hand to her chest and laughed. "You scared me. I didn't know you guys were home from school."

"We just got here." With a toss of her long blond hair, Vanessa crossed the room to the window and peered out. "So, are we going?"

Sofia closed the diary and smiled at her pretty elder daughter. "Of course. Why wouldn't we?"

"I heard it was going to snow." Despite the brutal cold of February in Vermont, Vanessa wore a plaid miniskirt, the navy blue wool tights underneath her only concession to the season.

In contrast, Sofia wore corduroy trousers with long johns underneath and a wool sweater over a turtleneck. She couldn't get over her kids' metabolisms. None of them appeared to be bothered by the frigid weather.

"I think we're just supposed to have flurries." Hoisting herself out of the armchair, Sofia carried the diary back to the trunk. "Are you excited about working on the auction?"

Catherine Stanley's upcoming charity auction featured part of her extensive antique jewelry collection. Sofia's task was to make hot and cold hors d'oeuvres and baked nibbles for a hundred people.

Vanessa grinned. "I'm incredibly excited. I still can't believe Julie chose me as her intern and we get to work on such a fun project."

Julie Butler worked for the marketing and public relations firm Catherine had hired to promote the high-profile event. Vanessa's internship duties included preparing the graphic art for the catalog and other materials.

Sofia latched the trunk and headed for the door, followed by her daughter.

"You inspire me, Mom," Vanessa said as they trooped downstairs. "I've been watching you research the stories from the quilt, and I'm going to do the same thing for the catalog."

Sofia was touched. Praise from a teen was high praise indeed. At the foot of the stairs, she gave Vanessa an impulsive hug. "That's great, sweetie. Let's talk about it more after we see the collection."

Vanessa hugged her back, then broke away. "Do I have time for a snack?"

The clatter from the kitchen informed Sofia that her other three children were already foraging. "Sure. I think I'll join you."

"Hi, Mom," said Wynter, her fifteen-year-old, as they entered the kitchen. "Can I make hot chocolate?" She was poised beside the cabinet where the cocoa box was stored, hope written on her face.

Matthew, a rambunctious ten-year-old, slid across the polished floor in his socks and bumped into his mother. "Hot chocolate!"

Sofia put an arm around her son and squeezed his shoulders. "I'm not sure you need any more sugar today."

"Aww, come on, Mom." Matthew gave her his most pitiful look. "I'll go outside and run around to burn it off."

Twelve-year-old Luke snorted. "Burn it off? Where did you get that?" He pulled the peanut butter down from the cupboard and started spreading it on celery sticks, frowning at Wynter when she grabbed one. Fergus, their border collie, sat nearby, waiting hopefully for a dropped treat.

Matthew pointed at Vanessa. "From her. She's always talking about burning off calories."

Sofia put up a hand. "Okay, go ahead and make hot chocolate, Wynter. Make a cup for me too."

"And me," Vanessa said. "What else do we have? I'm starving." She opened the pantry door and stared inside.

Sofia checked the thermometer outside the kitchen window. *Brrr. Twenty degrees. Even colder than a couple of hours ago.* "Vanessa and I are going out to Lake Lucy for a meeting, so can you keep an eye on the Crock-Pot, Wynter?" She had put together a beef stew earlier in the day, knowing that she would be away during normal supper preparation time. Her husband, Jim, often stepped in to help with meals, but he had a faculty meeting after school.

Wynter pulled a gallon of milk out of the refrigerator. "Will you be back for supper?"

"Of course." Sofia grabbed a bag of homemade rolls out of the freezer. "We can have these with the stew. Set the oven at 350, and wrap them in foil. Twenty minutes should do it."

"Will do." Wynter carefully measured milk into a saucepan.

Matthew darted over to his mother and hugged her around the waist. "Good luck on your trip, Mom."

Vanessa laughed. "We're just going to Lake Lucy, Matthew. What can possibly go wrong?" She pulled a rice cake out of a bag and took a bite.

After Julie arrived, they headed out in the family Suburban, Sofia at the wheel, Julie in the passenger seat, and Vanessa navigating from the back. Lake Lucy was on the outskirts of Cabot Falls, and after driving past fields and woods covered with snow, they turned onto the road leading to the lake. During the drive out of town, Sofia shared with Julie and Vanessa what she had learned so far about Beatrice Alice Kimble and her life in the Yorkshire moors.

Negotiating the tangle of narrow dirt lanes surrounding the lake, Sofia wished she had more of the luck Matthew had bestowed on her. She slowed for a welcome—but rare—road sign. "What does that say, Vanessa?"

Vanessa craned her head to look. "Shore Road." In the rearview mirror Sofia saw her daughter glance at the directions in her lap. "Turn right." Since cell phone coverage was spotty in much of the Vermont countryside, Sofia had brought along a paper printout.

Sofia took the turn carefully. The frozen dirt road was rutted and icy, making it difficult to maneuver the large vehicle. She had to creep along and use the brakes sparingly; one false move and they would slide off into the trees. Light snow had begun to fall, making the driving even more treacherous.

"I'd like to go to the Yorkshire moors." Julie gave a huge sigh.

With a green angora hat trimmed in faux fur perched on her red curls, she looked both warm and beautiful. "Just the name of the place evokes ruined castles and mysterious dark heroes, like in a Gothic romance."

"Do you think our ancestor lived in a castle?" Vanessa asked. "That would be so cool."

"I don't know yet," Sofia said. "What I've read so far said that she went to Yorkshire on business for the National Gallery." She switched on the wipers to combat the snow, which was thickening. So much for the forecast of flurries.

"In 1850?" Julie's eyes widened. "I'm impressed. Women weren't very prominent in the art world then, were they?"

"I don't think so," Sofia said. "I guess we'll have to ask Marla." They both laughed, since their friend was head librarian at Cabot Falls Library and loved doing research. If Marla didn't know the answer already, she'd know where to look for it.

Camps and houses began to appear on both sides of the road, giving Sofia faith that they were on the right track. Most of the dwellings were seasonal, with shutters over the windows and snow covering roofs and driveways. Some people had built year-round houses, and Catherine Stanley was one such resident.

As if echoing Sofia's thoughts, Julie said, "I'm surprised Catherine still lives way out here, now that her second husband has passed. It's lonely in winter."

Sofia felt a pang of sympathy. "She's a widow? I didn't know that." *How sad.* She knew she would be devastated to lose Jim.

"I wouldn't know about it either, but Catherine is an old college friend of my mother's. Mom told me all about it." Julie frowned. "Apparently he drowned in the lake."

"Lake Lucy?" Sofia was startled. "Then I am really surprised she stayed. She must think about him every time she looks out the window."

"Gruesome," Vanessa said.

Sofia slowed as they neared another road sign, and she struggled to read it through the thickening snow. "What street are we looking for, Vanessa?"

"Mallard Lane, Mom. This is it. Turn left here."

"Thanks for keeping me on track," Sofia said. "I've never met Catherine, Julie. You said she is a well-known philanthropist."

Julie laughed. "I'll say. She gave a million dollars to the new pediatric wing at the hospital in Burlington last year. The jewelry auction proceeds are going to support that too."

"Does she have children?" Sofia wondered if there was some tragedy in the woman's life that led her to support that particular charity.

"One son that I know of. Richard. I think he stays with her frequently. He came with her to our initial meeting at my office."

"How old is he?" Vanessa asked.

Julie shrugged. "Oh, about forty."

"Ugh. And he still hangs around with his mother? Lame." Vanessa's tone was decisive.

"I'm glad you have that philosophy," Sofia teased, glancing at her daughter in the rearview mirror. "I'm going to turn your room into an art studio when you move out."

"Gee, thanks, Mom. I'm glad you're eager for me to leave."

Actually the opposite was true. Sofia had never believed in empty-nest syndrome, but just the thought of Vanessa living elsewhere made her choke up.

"Your mom was joking," Julie said. "She'll be a wreck when you go off to college."

Her daughter's head disappeared from the mirror. *Probably hiding a grin,* Sofia thought, *or pretending to study the directions.* Then Vanessa squeaked in alarm. "Oh no! I gave you the wrong directions. We were supposed to take a different left.

Not Mallard Lane—Mallard Loop, but I can't see where that is."

"Let's call Catherine." Julie dug around in her purse for her cell phone. "Darn it. I don't have any bars."

"Me neither," Vanessa said. She moved her phone around in the air above her head, attempting to pick up a signal.

"Let me see the printout." Julie reached her hand toward Vanessa in the backseat. "I know my way around here a little."

Sofia slowed to a crawl, looking for a place to turn the bulky vehicle around. With most driveways blocked by two feet of snow, that would be a difficult proposition. Meanwhile, gusts of wind shook the pine trees, and the flakes became a heavy veil.

2

The Yorkshire Moors,
April 1850

"I think we are lost." Joseph Norris spoke in a somber tone edged with malice.

"Why do you say that?" Beatrice Alice Kimble turned from staring out the carriage window to address her companion, a smug young man of twenty-five. The art appraiser was her greatest rival and a reluctant colleague on her National Gallery assignment at Blackwell Castle.

Joseph gestured at the open expanse of moorland, silent and empty under the evening sky. "We have been traveling for miles. It seems we will never get there."

"Surely the driver knows his way. Lord Blackwell sent him to meet us."

They had taken the train from London that morning to the bustling little seaport of Whitby, North Yorkshire. From there, the driver headed northwest into the moors on a road that was little more than two ruts in the heather.

Beatrice could tell her common sense annoyed Joseph. With her tiny stature, sweet face, and shy demeanor, Beatrice knew men of her acquaintance often underestimated her—something she tried to use to her advantage. What had he expected? That she would have a fit of the vapors and call for smelling salts?

Joseph tried again. "Haven't you heard of the barghest? He's a black ghost dog with red eyes that preys on travelers." He grinned fiendishly. "Whitby is one of his haunts."

"Well, he can stay there." Beatrice turned to gaze out the window again, hoping Joseph would stop trying to scare her. He really was asinine.

The sky was almost fully black now, and thickening clouds hid the stars. Mist began to drift across the landscape, winding its way around trees and rock formations.

Despite her brave words, she felt a shiver of unease. She could well understand how the brooding landscape, so inhospitable to humans, gave rise to legends. Unless you knew your way, it would be extremely easy to become lost and stumble into a windy pit or a bog. There were human dangers too. Highwaymen were known to roam the moors, eager to take advantage of unwary and defenseless strangers.

She had never ventured so far from London, from her comfortable home with Horatio Kimble, her guardian. He had taken her in when she was an orphan of six, and he and his late wife had shown her nothing but kindness.

More than that, he had trained her to appraise art, even to discern forgeries. As a trustee of the National Gallery, he was in charge of locating and obtaining pieces for their collection in hopes of someday rivaling the Louvre in Paris. And now, for the first time, it was Beatrice who was responsible for assessing paintings for possible purchase.

She thought back to the night Horatio had made the assignment, a cold and rainy evening just the previous month.

"I don't see why Beatrice should bother herself with a trip to Yorkshire, Horatio." Joseph had rested one polished boot on the fireplace fender and crossed his arms. As usual, he sat in the best chair, hogging the warmth from the fire. "The weather up there is miserable this time of year."

It wasn't much better in London. Outside the tightly drawn velvet drapes, rain beat against the windows, lending the dimly lit room a snug, cozy air.

Seated at his desk, a folio of papers in front of him, Horatio adjusted his spectacles—so he could better study the young man, Beatrice assumed. "I am sending Beatrice because she is the foremost expert on Renaissance art in London." He smiled wryly. "And that includes Theodore and myself. I owe it to the National Gallery to seek her opinion."

Fellow trustee Theodore Sedgwick harrumphed, seeming to disagree with Horatio's assessment of Beatrice's skills as being superior to his. His words, however, were conciliatory. "Horatio is right, Joseph. Together, you and Beatrice will make a formidable team. We need a proper assessment of Lord Blackwell's collection so we can pay an appropriate price." Theodore sat on the other side of the fire, his bulk almost overwhelming the dainty armchair he had accepted with reluctance. Once in a while, he glanced at Joseph's capacious seat, obviously longing to be there instead.

"And we need Blackwell's collection badly," Horatio said. "The gallery hasn't acquired a single piece for three years. If this state of affairs continues, I've heard rumors the trustees may be stripped of their powers."

"That's right," Theodore said. "They're bandying about the appointment of a director in the House of Commons." He shuddered. "One man they are considering isn't even an Englishman."

The other two men burst into vociferous debate at Theodore's words, and Beatrice, huddled in a wing chair in the corner of the room near the bookcases, smiled at their passion. Gallery politics wasn't her area of concern or interest. Let men argue and squabble. For her, it was all about the paintings, and despite her carefully indifferent exterior, a rising triumph and joy threatened to bubble over. Evaluating Lord Blackwell's collection, including the fabled

Madonna of the Garden by legendary painter Vittore Biagio, would be the making of her career.

Once established, she wanted nothing more than to spend her days sharing the joy and delight she found in beautiful works of art with others. One notable feature of the gallery was its location in a part of London accessible to all, not only the rich or well-connected, a decision Beatrice heartily supported.

In light of her goals, she supposed she could put up with Joseph on the trip to Blackwell Castle. Horatio had confided that the trustees were reluctant to entrust the mission to her alone, so Joseph was coming along as a sop to quell their concerns.

Now, as she gazed at the Yorkshire countryside, a smile curved her lips. What a dent that information would put in his insufferable pride, should she be so bold as to share it.

Joseph again interrupted her thoughts. "Beatrice, what do you know about our esteemed client, Lord Blackwell?"

"Not much," she admitted. "But what do I need to know beyond the fact that he has a fine art collection?"

Joseph chuckled. "You have a lot to learn, my dear." He ignored her bristling at his condescending tone. "It is our job to ferret out everything we can about the owner of a piece."

She was taken aback by this statement. "Why is that? It sounds most intrusive."

He tapped the side of his nose. "Not only do we need to establish provenance—I assume you know what that is?"

"Of course. The origin of a painting or work of art and the chain of ownership. It's critical to establish provenance to avoid purchasing stolen or fraudulent works."

"Very good, Beatrice. You have been listening to your guardian."

"Naturally I . . ." She bit back the rest of her irritated words. It wouldn't do to show Joseph how much he got under her skin. "So what do you know about the lord?" She made her tone challenging.

Joseph chuckled again. "He is a very interesting fellow. His family made their fortune in whaling, which is now regrettably in decline due to competition from other countries. He has interests in Castlerock Village, of course, and several farms, but his purse isn't what it used to be."

"Is that why he is selling?" It was an unfortunate turn of events, for certain. If she owned works of that caliber, she would be hard-pressed to let them go, but at least at the National Gallery, they would be enjoyed by thousands.

"Quite possibly. Unless he despises them. Renaissance art isn't everyone's cup of tea, you know."

She merely grunted in response to this bait. Beatrice knew Joseph favored baroque art, something she frankly didn't understand. It was far too florid and fanciful; hence the name baroque, she supposed.

Joseph paused, and when no further response was forthcoming, he continued. "I've heard rumors that smugglers ply these coasts . . . and art is among the items traveling illicitly."

Incredulity and anger suffused her chest with heat. "Are you implying that Blackwell is involved?" Accusing their client of criminal acts was well beyond the pale.

Joseph held up a quelling hand. "Of course not. I've heard things, that's all. And it's better to be aware rather than hoodwinked."

"You are too much, Joseph. Please keep your miserable speculations to yourself."

He refused to be deterred. "Don't be naive, Beatrice. Not everyone is as upright as your guardian." He made that sound like a bad thing. "Blackwell's personal life is equally as fraught with questions. His wife, Lily, died mysteriously." He paused again. "At least, that is the story. Something's wrong there; I have it on good authority."

This vile gossip was beyond what she could bear. "Joseph—" Before she could continue scolding him for sharing this unseemly gossip, the carriage gave a lurch, sending her careening across the seat into odious and mortifying contact with his person.

"What the—" Joseph did his best to separate them as the carriage jerked again and then stopped entirely. "Has the driver gone mad?"

Grasping the ceiling strap, Beatrice slid back to her side of the carriage as best she could on the slanted, slippery leather seat. Her eyes wildly searched the darkness for some clue to explain the calamity.

Joseph fumbled for the door handle. "I'm going to give him a piece of my mind!" He finally got the door unlatched and began to edge his way out gingerly, using the edge of the entrance to prevent himself from tumbling into the ditch.

And then a shot rang out.

3

Cabot Falls, Vermont,
Present Day

*W*ith relief and gratitude, Sofia turned the Suburban into Catherine's driveway, which was marked by a mailbox painted with her last name. They had been forced to retrace their steps to find Mallard Loop, a difficult prospect since snow-covered pine branches obscured the sign. In addition, visibility was reduced to almost nil by the snow and gusting wind.

I'm exhausted and drained, and I haven't even had the meeting yet.

Julie echoed Sofia's thoughts with a huge sigh. "Gosh, I'm tired. And I wasn't driving. Good job, Sofia."

"We're not there yet," Sofia said with a laugh. Both hands firmly on the wheel, she navigated the drive's steep, winding hill, the Suburban fishtailing a little. Finally they reached the crest, where an enormous post-and-beam house sat, lights glittering in the foyer windows that stretched to the second floor.

"Wow," Vanessa said. "This place is huge." A familiar white van was parked in front of the four-car garage. "What is Ethan's dad doing here?"

The logo of David Hall's security company was painted on the van's side and back. The amount of snow covering the vehicle revealed it had been parked there awhile.

Sofia pulled to a stop beside the van and turned off the engine.

"I wouldn't be surprised if Catherine has a security system. Her jewelry collection is really valuable."

Julie's eyes were on the house as she opened the passenger door. "What a gorgeous house. I bet she has a stupendous view of the lake from up here."

They gathered their belongings and trudged along the snowy path to the flagstone front porch. Through the windows, Sofia could see a great room with crystal chandeliers and a huge stone fireplace. She rang the bell.

A few moments later, a slender woman with short, curly blond hair opened the front door. She wore pale blue wool slacks and a matching cashmere sweater, giving the impression of elegant comfort.

"Come on in," she said, holding the door wide. She glanced at the glowering sky, still dumping snow. "It's a miserable day out there."

"I'm sorry we're late," Sofia said. "We got lost."

"Most people do the first time. Come in and warm up."

They obeyed, stamping their feet to get rid of the snow before entering the house. "I'm Catherine Stanley," the woman said as they took off their coats and boots. After Sofia, Julie, and Vanessa introduced themselves, she showed them where to put their garments. "Stocking feet are fine." She pointed to her own feet, clad in woolly socks.

Catherine led them into the great room, to a grouping of three leather sofas and a large, ornate coffee table arranged in a semicircle in front of a roaring fireplace. They set down their totes and folders on the table. Then, as one, they stepped closer to the fireplace to warm up, stretching their hands to the crackling, sweet-smelling flames.

"You have a lovely home," Sofia said. The great room ended in another wall of windows with two porches beyond, one open and the other screened. The white circle of Lake Lucy lay below, surrounded by pines and bare trees, an occasional cottage or camp peeking out.

"Thank you," Catherine said graciously. "My late husband and I designed it." A brief shadow crossed her face, but her tone was cheerful when she asked, "What can I get you? Coffee? Tea? Water or soda? I have to finish up with some workmen, and then I'm all yours."

"We know the Halls," Vanessa said, blushing.

"She's dating David's son," Julie said, sending the teenager a teasing smile.

"Really? Ethan's here, if you want to say hi, Vanessa."

"That's okay. I'll wait until they're done." She plopped down on one of the sofas, joined by Sofia and Julie. The women asked for coffee while Vanessa just wanted water, and Catherine headed off to the kitchen with a promise to be back soon.

Sofia leaned back and gazed up at the soaring wood beams framing the space. Behind their seats, a staircase wound up to the second floor, which was edged by a balcony. Doors led off both sides of the great room. The one to the kitchen stood open, revealing glimpses of stainless steel appliances and hickory cabinets.

"I could get used to this," Julie said, wiggling her toes as she leaned back. Then she laughed and sat up. "But enough house envy." She reached into her tote. "Vanessa, I want you to look over the proposal so you can be familiar with it too." She handed Vanessa a sheaf of papers.

Sofia glanced over her own proposal. She had been struck with a creative idea while planning the menu. She hoped Catherine would like it.

The clatter of a tray announced their refreshments had arrived. However, it wasn't Catherine who brought them; it was a trim young woman with a glossy auburn bob.

"Hi," she said. "I'm Melanie, Catherine's assistant." She was as expensively dressed as Catherine, and small diamonds sparkled at her ears. She set the tray on the huge coffee table. "Help yourself. She said she'd just be a minute." With a pat to smooth her hair, she sashayed off.

A small pot held coffee. *A nice touch*, Sofia thought, and she poured mugs for Julie and herself. Vanessa's water even had ice and a slice of lemon. Sofia added cream to her coffee and took a sip. She could tell by the dark, rich brew that Catherine had discerning taste. She'd have to be sure to procure high-quality ingredients for the event.

The thump of footsteps pulled their attention to the staircase. A middle-aged man with a comb-over and a paunch clomped gracelessly down the stairs, his face lighting up when he spotted them.

"Hello there." He waved as he approached, joining them at the fireside by sitting on an ottoman that placed his back to the fire. "What brings you out to the boondocks in the middle of a snowstorm?"

I hope he's exaggerating, or we may have trouble getting home, Sofia thought. "We're here to discuss arrangements for the auction. I'm Sofia Parker." She introduced the others.

He stared at each face in turn as if memorizing their features. "Richard Brown, Catherine's son." His gaze dropped to the tray. "Coffee. That sounds like a good idea." Raising his voice, he bellowed, "Melanie! Melanie?"

The young woman appeared in the kitchen doorway, looking none too pleased at his summons. "What is it? I'm busy."

He pointed at the tray. "Be a love and bring me a cup?" His attempt to sound charming apparently fell flat because she scowled in response and disappeared. If there had been a thought balloon over her head, Sofia was sure it would have read, *I don't work for you.*

Richard turned his attention to Sofia's folder, picking it up and riffling through the pages. She managed to restrain herself from snatching it out of his hands since offending the client's son was probably not a good move. Fortunately Melanie reappeared with a mug, forcing him to put down the folder. She then thrust the mug unceremoniously into Richard's hands before scurrying off. He took a sip and set it down—right on top of the folder.

"Uh, excuse me, Mr. Brown, but that's my folder, and I need to look it over."

"Oh, sure. And please, call me Richard." He moved his cup and handed her the documents. After taking an additional sip, he glanced around the group again. "So, what do you think about this auction?" By his tone, it was difficult to tell if he was happy about it.

Sofia and Julie looked at each other. Julie nodded slightly as if to say she would field this one. She put on a gleaming smile and tossed her bright curls. Julie in professional mode was an invincible force. "We think it's wonderful. We're going to do everything we can to make it a huge success so it will raise a lot of money to help build that pediatrics wing."

"That's right," Vanessa said. "I hate to think about those poor, sick little kids. I have three younger siblings myself." She shuddered. "I'd hate it if something happened to them."

"Lucky you." Richard picked at the fingernails of his left hand. "Some of us aren't so fortunate."

Vanessa looked stricken. "I'm sorry," she mumbled.

Sofia stuffed down a surge of irritation at his rudeness and wracked her brain for a tactful but assertive response. Before she could formulate one, he spoke again. "The whole thing is my fault, you know."

The trio sat silent, not sure how to respond. "Uh, I'm not

sure what you mean," Sofia finally said. Apparently this charity auction was a minefield of family dynamics, and they had stepped heedlessly into it.

He kept his head lowered. "I had a twin. But he died at birth. That's why my mother is so hot on this children's wing. She regards it as a penance for her wrongs."

Oh my. What an odd thing to say. At the same time, Sofia felt extreme sorrow for Catherine. The poor woman had certainly suffered her share of tragedy. By the way Julie shifted around on the sofa beside her, Sofia guessed she shared her concern and discomfort.

Fortunately, voices in the other room announced Catherine's return. She entered the great room accompanied by David Hall; his lanky, handsome, dark-haired son; and another man. Ethan grinned when he spotted Vanessa, and she practically twinkled with joy in response.

Sofia had known Vanessa starting to date was inevitable, and she was thankful her daughter's first boyfriend was a nice, reliable young man with plans for his future.

"I'm so glad you did those upgrades to the system," Catherine said as she and her companions approached the others. "I'll sleep easier."

"I'm still not certain what happened," David said, frowning. "The alarm should have gone off."

"These things happen," the other man said. "We get power outages all the time out here." At first glance, with his buzz cut, tattooed hands, and broad, weathered face, he stood out like a sore thumb in his elegant surroundings. Even his voice was harsh, with an undercurrent of South Boston.

David didn't look satisfied by this explanation. "Well, we'll be monitoring it to be sure it doesn't do that again." He turned to his son. "Ready to head out?"

"Sure, Dad. I just want to say hi to Vanessa."

The older Hall smiled his agreement, giving a wave to Sofia and Julie. He and Catherine continued to confer as they strolled toward the door, the other man trailing along behind. Ethan hunkered down beside Vanessa, and from what Sofia could hear, they were discussing the upcoming Winter Carnival. Vanessa was competing for Carnival Queen.

"There was an intruder here the other night," David said, explaining the exchange to Sofia and Julie.

"Yes," Richard said, "and it's a good thing I happened to come downstairs and scared him off."

"Really? That's awful." Sofia shuddered at the idea of an intruder. Had the prowler been after the jewelry collection?

"David's the best at security systems," Julie said stoutly, as if worried that their friend's skills and reputation might be maligned. "He even does the local banks."

"I'm sure he is," Richard said. "But even the best system can be breached." He narrowed his eyes, watching as his mother concluded her discussion with David and the other man.

"Who's that with your mother and David?" Sofia asked.

"Gil Masters. He's our chauffeur and 'handyman.'" Richard emphasized this last role by making quote marks with his fingers.

A less likely employee for Catherine Sofia couldn't imagine, but perhaps the wealthy woman had a reason to employ a man who looked tough. Maybe she felt safer with him around. *Where was he when the intruder broke in, I wonder?*

The Halls left, and Catherine finally turned her attention to her visitors. "I see you've met Dickie."

Her son rolled his eyes. "Please, Mother, call me Richard."

"I'm sorry, dear," Catherine said. "Old habits die hard."

"I know what you mean," Sofia said. "My kids hate it when I use pet names." She couldn't imagine still doing that when they were adults, though. Had the loss of Richard's twin made it difficult for Catherine to accept that her son was grown up?

Catherine's tone became brisk. "Before we get started, would you like to see the jewelry collection?"

With the light fading outside and the snow continuing to fall, Sofia wanted nothing more at this point than to have the meeting and leave. Julie and Vanessa seemed eager to see the collection, though, so she swallowed her impatience and followed Catherine to another room on the first floor. Melanie, who had returned from the kitchen, accompanied them, but the two men disappeared, apparently intent on their own business.

Catherine punched numbers into a keypad to open the safe room, then switched on a light. Dozens of tiny spotlights came on all over the windowless room, like stars popping out at night.

In unison, the visitors caught their breath as the gems sparkled and gleamed. The fabulous collection filled cases on three sides of the room and a few displays in the center.

"I had no idea your collection was so extensive," Sofia said. Everywhere she looked, she saw the dazzle of diamonds, the glitter of emeralds and rubies, and the rich, soft glow of pearls.

"My great-grandmother started it," Catherine said, "back in the 1880s." She led the way to the center of the room. The case in pride of place contained just three pieces, but all were diamond brooches with elaborate floral designs. One looked like a bouquet of flowers, another a spray, and the third was a cascade bouquet, with strands of flowers dripping down from a central grouping.

"These are called corsage brooches," Catherine said. "You can guess why."

Vanessa placed her hand on the area of her chest where a corsage would be pinned. "Wow. They are stunning."

Catherine smiled. "I find them a bit gaudy myself, but right now they are the most valuable pieces I own, believe it or not."

She led them to another case. "These are my personal favorites." The pins and necklaces depicted little pictures in bright colors—birds, flowers, and landscapes.

"Are they enamel?" Julie asked.

"Close. They are called micromosaics, and they're made of incredibly tiny pieces of glass. Most of them are from Italy. Ladies of the Victorian era loved to collect them." She pointed to a rectangular pin showing a bouquet of pink roses on an indigo background. "This one is from about 1850. The artisan used a technique called *millefiori*. Each flower is actually cut from a cane of glass with the pattern embedded."

"'Thousand flowers,'" Sofia translated. *Did Beatrice get to wear a millefiori pin? I might never find out, but it's fun to think so.*

Catherine looked at Sofia in surprise. "*Parli italiano?*"

"*Parlo un po.* I speak a little. I've been brushing up so I can translate a diary my grandmother left me."

"That's very interesting. You'll have to tell me more sometime." Catherine led the way toward the doorway. "Right now, let's discuss the auction plans."

They reconvened back in the great room over fresh cups of coffee. Catherine and Julie discussed the range of tasks her firm would handle for the auction, including invitations, publicity, media, and the preparation of the catalog, posters, and Web content. Vanessa took notes, and when Sofia glanced over, she saw her daughter was already doodling designs for the materials.

Sofia listened with one ear, her uneasiness growing with each passing moment. Outside the tall windows, snow swirled and danced in the glow of the outdoor lights. Night had fallen, which meant a dark as well as slippery ride home.

"Sofia, let's see your menu," Catherine finally said. Despite the early evening hour, the older woman was bright-eyed and energetic.

With relief, Sofia picked up the folder and handed it to her page by page as she explained. "After I learned that most of your jewelry could be characterized as Victorian, I decided to carry that through to the food."

"What a great idea." Catherine's face reflected her approval as she read the list of food ideas. "Tiny beef Wellingtons, ham on biscuits, cucumber sandwiches, angels on horseback—what are those?"

"Oysters wrapped in bacon."

"Yum!" Vanessa burst out. She clapped her hand over her mouth. "Sorry. I guess I'm getting hungry."

Catherine laughed. "I can understand that." For the first time, she appeared to notice what time it was. "I'm so sorry I've kept you here this late." She shuffled the pages of the menu together. "This looks great, Sofia. Why don't we finalize it another day so you can get on the road?"

Sofia was disappointed at the delay in wrapping up the plans but was eager to get home so she didn't argue. "I can call you tomorrow. I think you'll like the desserts I've come up with."

"I'm sure I will." Catherine stood, smoothing down the front of her trousers.

"Catherine." Gil Masters came striding out from the kitchen. "I've been listening to the scanner. The snow is intensifying, and police are telling everyone to stay off the roads." He looked at Sofia and the others. "I'm afraid you ladies aren't going anywhere tonight."

4

The Yorkshire Moors,
April 1850

*B*eatrice cried out at the sound of the gunshot, which was followed swiftly by a second. "What was that?" A sinking sensation in her belly told her she already knew the answer.

"I think we're being robbed." Joseph pulled himself back inside the carriage. "I'm not going out there." He tried to close the door, but it kept falling open.

Beatrice fumbled for the millefiori pin on her bodice; it had been made in Venice by the finest artisans. Horatio had given it to her on her twentieth birthday last fall, and it was one of her most precious possessions. Reluctant for it to fall into the clutches of a highwayman, she unpinned it, closed the clasp, and slipped it down her bodice.

Just in time. A bulky figure appeared in the doorway of the coach, and by the light of the lanterns, Beatrice saw he wore a mask. A hat pulled low over his brow disguised the color and cut of his hair. He was clean-shaven.

He glanced up to the driver. "You stay where you are," he said before turning his attention to Beatrice and Joseph. "Get out, both of you."

Joseph cringed backward, reaching into his waistcoat pocket. "Take my watch. Take my money. Just don't hurt me."

The robber reached for Joseph's arm and tugged. "Out."

Whining and pleading, Joseph allowed himself to be pulled from the carriage. Then the man reached for Beatrice.

Although she had never known such acute terror, several close calls on the streets of London had taught Beatrice to never show fear. Taking a deep breath to still her racing heart, she slid across the seat toward the man. Perhaps if they cooperated, the ordeal would soon be over.

Her plan to remain calm came to naught when he jerked her out of the carriage so roughly that he hurt her arm, almost pulling it from its socket. She cried out in pain, and the man clapped his gloved hand over her mouth. "Hush yer bawling, missy."

The thick wool glove smelled foul, of fish and tobacco. Beatrice squirmed and wiggled, managing to kick the man hard in the knee with the heel of her boot. As a result, he moved his hand enough that she was able to fasten her teeth into his tender wrist. He staggered back in pain, swearing. "Do something, you fools!" she yelled to Joseph and the coachman.

Before they could respond, the thunder of hooves was heard. Three horsemen carrying torches approached, the lead figure a man of about thirty years, dressed in a long cloak and seated astride a tall black stallion.

"Hallo there!" the leader called. "What's going on?"

The highwayman stumbled for his mount, a shaggy pony, and threw himself on top of it. Then he wheeled away, not heeding the cries to halt. At a gesture from the leader, the other two men tore after the robber, guns drawn.

"Are you all right?" The leader slid down from his horse and strode over to Beatrice, who was rubbing her shoulder. "Did that brute hurt you?"

"I'm all right. A little sore, but it's not dislocated." She gazed up at the man, the flickering lantern casting shadows on his chiseled cheekbones and square jaw. His dark, deep-set eyes were filled with concern. Having ascertained that she was intact, he swept off his hat. "Lord Blackwell at your service. I assume you are Miss Kimble?"

"That is correct." She sketched a curtsy. "Thank you for coming to our rescue, my lord."

"I'm glad I did. The roads have been plagued with blackguards lately, and once it fell dark, I thought I should come find you." He nodded at Joseph, who had come to join them. The men introduced themselves and shook hands.

"Let's get you on your way." He turned to the coachman. "We need to get this rig back on the road. Did the wheel break?"

"I don't think so, my lord." He pointed. "We hit that rock, and it sent us off the verge into a boggy ditch."

How fortunate that Lord Blackwell came this way at this particular time, Beatrice reflected. Otherwise, it didn't bear thinking about.

Joseph joined Blackwell and the driver in examining the tilted carriage, and when the other men returned, they managed to set it back on the track. Then Beatrice and Joseph climbed aboard, and the driver set off behind their escort. Beatrice curled into her corner, consumed with relief that they had escaped harm.

"Well, that was a bit of excitement." Now that the danger was over, Joseph was relishing their adventure, conveniently forgetting his own cowardice.

"More excitement than I needed," she said. The temptation to tweak him for his poor behavior in the face of danger welled up, but she managed to squash it. *Why antagonize him?* "I'm just happy we're on our way to the castle, not slung across the back of a pony on my way God knows where."

Joseph cocked a brow. "Do you really think he was after your virtue?" His tone implied that it wasn't very likely.

She bristled, as he had probably intended. Several retorts

came to mind, but she discarded them all. Working with Joseph was certainly going to be a test of her character. The man was entirely infuriating. "Then why did he grab hold of my person?" she asked mildly.

Joseph shrugged. "You probably weren't moving fast enough for him. I'm sure he just wanted your valuables, such as they are."

"That's right. I left the gold and diamonds at home." Beatrice allowed a trace of sarcasm to enter her tone.

Fortunately for Beatrice's nerves, the remainder of the journey was short. They soon turned off the trail and passed through towering stone posts bordered by gatehouses. The entrance to Blackwell Castle. One of the servants dismounted and shut the wrought iron gate behind them with a piercing squeak.

The ancient castle loomed ahead, a pile of battlements and towers with a central keep, where lights glowed invitingly.

"What a forbidding old heap," Joseph said. "I'll bet more than one ghost roams those halls, chains clanking."

Biting her tongue, Beatrice remained silent as the carriage pulled up in front of a massive door fronted with stone steps. Every bone and muscle ached after the interminable journey. She hoped the lord's hospitality extended to a comfortable bed.

One of the servants came to open their door, and after giving his reins to another, Lord Blackwell escorted them into the great hall, the main room of the keep.

By its stone walls and floor, arched windows, and huge fireplace, Beatrice could tell this was the oldest part of the castle. The room was icy cold because of the lofty ceiling with its second-floor gallery, and she looked longingly toward the roaring fire. In the flickering torchlight, several tapestries glowed softly. They, too, looked ancient. To her right, a stone staircase wound upward in two flights.

A woman wearing a black dress and holding a candlestick waddled through a door and came toward them. As she drew closer, Beatrice noted she wore her hair entirely scraped back flat to her head, a style most unflattering to her round face.

"Sarah," Lord Blackwell said. "Please join me in welcoming our guests, Miss Kimble and Mr. Norris."

She nodded curtly. "Come with me, and I'll show you to your rooms."

"After you freshen up, meet me in the drawing room, which leads to the dining room, and we'll have a meal," the lord said as they headed in the direction of the staircase.

"I'd be glad to, if I can find it," Joseph said with a laugh. "You have a magnificent, if not monumental, home." To Beatrice's amusement, he gazed around as if in stunned admiration. She hadn't witnessed him fawning over a client before this.

Blackwell laughed in agreement. "That it is." He pointed to a door on the other side of the hall. "Through there is what we call the new wing, refurbished by my grandfather. The drawing room is immediately to your right. See you there in an hour?"

Following the dour Sarah, they climbed the stairs, an act Beatrice was sure would finish her off entirely. The housekeeper pointed the way to Joseph's room, then did the courtesy of escorting Beatrice to hers, down the opposite hallway. As far as she could tell, she was in the new wing, above the dining room. Here the hallway was carpeted with a rich Persian rug, and gold-flocked wallpaper clothed the plaster walls.

Beatrice's room was about halfway down the hall, a large chamber with a canopied four-poster bed and massive wardrobe and bureau. A small fire burning in a tiled fireplace provided an oasis of warmth, and the soothing, rhythmic sound of the waves came through the open casements. She had seen the sea only once, when her guardians had taken her on a holiday to Brighton.

"I wanted to air it out for you," Sarah explained as Beatrice crossed the room to the windows, wanting to peer out although full night had fallen. Tendrils of mist drifted like twisting ropes in the air, touched by the light shining out from the lamps beside the bed and on the mantel.

A housemaid barged through the half-open door, a pitcher of steaming water in her hands. She sloshed it into a basin, sliding her gaze sideways to study Beatrice.

"Hello," Beatrice said. "Thank you for bringing that. I could use a wash." She laughed, but the maid didn't respond to her overture. Instead, she thumped the pitcher down and scurried out.

"Don't mind Ettie; she's a trifle touched." Sarah moved toward the doorway. "I'll leave you to freshen up, unless you need a hand?" She gestured toward Beatrice's clothing.

"Oh. Does the lord dress for dinner?" Beatrice glanced around. Her trunk hadn't yet made it to her room.

"Not tonight. No, he won't stand on ceremony. So you'll be all right." With that assurance, Sarah picked up her candlestick and left Beatrice to her own devices.

The first thing she did once the door was locked was open her bodice to rescue her pin. Then she washed up, brushing and pinning up her hair using the silver set on the bureau.

According to the mantel clock, she still had half an hour before dinner, but rather than lie down—and not get up until morning—she decided to explore the room. The main part of the wardrobe was empty, but when she brushed her hand across the shelf, she touched something soft and startling. With a shout, she jumped back.

Was there a creature up there? A knock came at the door. One of the servants stood there, her trunk resting on his broad shoulder. "Where do you want this, miss?"

She pointed to the carpet next to the wardrobe. "Thank you for lugging that up here. What's your name?"

He touched his forelock. "Sam, miss. Is there anything else?"

She debated asking, then went ahead. "Can you check the

wardrobe shelf for me, please? There is something there, but I can't reach it."

Without question, he thrust his hand into the wardrobe and ran his fingers along the shelf. "This what you're looking for?" He held a mourning fan made of black ostrich feathers, unattractive but far from threatening. Still, its presence was a grim reminder that death had touched this house. *As any house this age, of course,* she reminded herself.

She waved her hand. "You can put it back. I felt it when I was reaching around and wasn't quite sure what it was. It gave me quite a start. I thought it was a mouse."

"No mice up here, miss. The cat takes care of them."

"That's good to know."

He slid the fan back onto the shelf, and then, with another tug of his forelock, he was gone.

Beatrice knelt and unlocked her trunk. Unpacking could wait until morning, but she needed to find a shawl. Judging by the rest of the house, no doubt the dining room would be dank and chilly. She chose one of fine merino wool in lavender that looked nice with her navy blue dress. Then she took one last glance in the mirror, tucked a stray piece of hair into place, and headed down to her first dinner in a real castle.

Lord Blackwell and Joseph stood when she entered the drawing room, which was elegantly appointed with ornate rococo plasterwork and gilded French furniture. The contrast between the rustic, ancient keep and this lavish room was startling.

"Ah, Miss Kimble." Blackwell bowed. "I trust you found everything to your satisfaction." He wore well-cut tweed that suited his rangy but broad-shouldered build.

"Yes, thank you." A golden-hued painting of fishing boats placed over the marble mantel caught her attention. "Is that a Dutch master?"

"That's right." Blackwell gazed up at the canvas. "You have a good eye." He went on to discuss the provenance of the painting while Joseph looked on impatiently.

Beatrice could feel Joseph's displeasure at being ignored like arrows in her back. Hoping to placate him, she said, "Mr. Norris helped acquire some splendid Dutch works for the gallery."

Blackwell politely turned to Joseph. "Is that so? Tell me about them."

Before Joseph could answer, a tall, cadaverous man appeared in the doorway. "Dinner is served, my lord."

"Very good, Wesley." Blackwell held his arm out to Beatrice. "Shall we?"

In the vast dining room, which was decorated much like the drawing room, Beatrice saw to her relief that their places were set at one end, near the fireplace. Seated with a view of the crackling fire, she was content to dine on hearty barley soup and roast mutton while half listening to the men talk. Slouched in his chair like he owned the place, Joseph held center stage, proud as a peacock of his knowledge and expertise regarding art.

Blackwell listened as he ate, making comments now and then. During a lull in Joseph's spiel, he turned to Beatrice. "Your specialty is Italian Renaissance works, is it not?"

"Yes, it is. I enjoy art from most eras, but there is something special about the Renaissance. Perhaps it is the fact that it represents a rebirth of creativity after the Dark Ages." She also had Italian ancestors, which gave her a deep sense of kinship with artists from that country, but her personal history wasn't something she readily shared with strangers.

"True. The barbarian hordes made it their business to destroy art and manuscripts along with the remains of the Roman Empire," Blackwell said. "We have a ruined abbey on our grounds. After it was raided and burned, villagers stole most of the stones. But the arches remain."

"I'd like to see it," Beatrice said. "I often find a melancholy beauty in ruined places." She leaned back so Wesley could take away her decidedly empty plate.

Joseph hid a snort behind his wineglass. He had no patience for sentiment, Beatrice knew.

"I'll make sure you visit the abbey and other sites of interest while you are here," Blackwell said. "Does such a pursuit interest you, Mr. Norris?"

Joseph shrugged. "Perhaps. If I have time." He twirled his wineglass, his other arm resting over the back of his chair. "Appraisals can take much longer than most people realize."

Blackwell cocked his head, regarding Joseph closely. "Do you have relatives in the area, Mr. Norris?"

Joseph stopped moving the glass. "I think not." He gave a short bark of laughter. "I'm London born and bred."

"Of course. It's just for a minute there you reminded me of someone." Blackwell put his napkin beside his plate. "Since there are only three of us, let's dispense with the usual port and cigars in the billiards room while our lone lady withdraws." He grinned at Beatrice, and for a moment, she caught her breath at how handsome he was. She hadn't seen him smile before, she realized.

She set down her own napkin. "I'm for bed, if you gentlemen don't mind. It's been a long day." *And a strange one.*

Once upstairs, Beatrice gratefully submitted to the maid's help in unlacing her stays, then dismissed her with a request for tea in the morning. Clad in a long white gown, she brushed her hair by the open window, then climbed into the comfortable bed, the sound of the sea lulling her into slumber.

Hours later, in the dark of night, her eyes flew open. *What was that?* Something had jolted her out of sleep. She held her breath and listened.

There it was again. A baby's heartbreaking, relentless cry.

5

Cabot Falls, Vermont,
Present Day

$\mathcal{C}$atherine Stanley glanced out the picture windows, which now framed a view of driving snow. "I had no idea it was getting so bad." She extended a hand to her visitors. "Maybe you should stay tonight. We have plenty of room."

Sofia's heart sank. While she liked her new client, the idea of having to spend the night at a virtual stranger's house was not appealing. The glum looks on Vanessa's and Julie's faces confirmed they felt the same. "Thank you for that kind invitation, Catherine. Let me call my husband first." She pulled out her cell phone. Only one bar.

Correctly guessing the problem, Catherine said, "We have a landline with an extension in the kitchen. Feel free to use that."

Gil led the way into the quiet space gleaming with stainless steel and granite. He pointed to a telephone on the counter below a row of cookbooks. "There's the phone. Better hurry up before the lines go down."

Startled, Sofia glanced at the handyman. His weather-beaten face was so impassive that she couldn't tell if he was serious. "Is that a problem out here?"

He nodded. The lights in the kitchen flickered. "See what I mean?" With another nod, he left her to use the phone.

Jim answered right away. "Sofia! Where are you?" By the

tension in his tone, she could tell he was worried. "Did you have trouble on the road?"

"No, we're all right. We're still at Catherine Stanley's."

The lights flickered again. Wouldn't that be the perfect topper to the day, to be stranded without electricity?

"You haven't left yet? Then you'd better stay. The roads are a mess, and the ones out by the lake are going to be a low priority for plowing and salting."

"You really think so, Jim?" She sighed. "I just want to be home." Longing twisted Sofia's heart as she pictured the family sitting around the dinner table, eating her beef stew, laughing and bantering.

"Think of it this way: If you go off the road and get stuck, how long will it be before anyone can get to you? The cell coverage is spotty, and most of the houses and cabins are closed up. You could be stranded all night."

He was right. She pictured the three of them huddled in the Suburban in a storm. They could easily freeze to death overnight. At best they would be extremely miserable.

She sighed again. "All right. We'll do that. But if we're not home by noon tomorrow, come looking for us."

"We'll touch base in the morning. The snow is supposed to stop in the wee hours, but you never know." Sofia heard children's voices in the background. "Hang on. The kids all want to say hi."

Sofia spoke to Matthew, Luke, and Wynter, then to Jim again before hanging up dejectedly. While some mothers enjoyed time away from their demanding families, she wasn't among them.

"Catherine, if the offer is still open, we'd love to stay," Sofia told her hostess when she rejoined the others in front of the fire. "Jim says it wouldn't be safe for us to try to get home tonight."

Vanessa gave a mock groan. "Darn it. I left my homework at home." She grinned at her mother.

"Of course," Catherine said. "I wouldn't feel right about it if you had trouble. It's pretty isolated out here."

Julie's face went white as the reality of their situation sank in. "I'd better call Mark. He and the twins are probably worried sick." Julie and her husband were parents to twelve-year-old Ellie and Cindy. "May I use the phone?" She got to her feet.

"Of course." Also rising, Catherine threw another log on the fire and poked the flames higher.

"It's on the counter near the cookbooks," Sofia said. She gathered her menus and put them back into her tote. Maybe they could discuss the rest of the menu in the morning and save another trip out here. Then she had an idea. "Catherine, I would love to cook dinner for you tonight, in appreciation for your hospitality."

The woman placed the poker back in its stand. "No thanks are necessary. It's a time-honored Vermont tradition to take in travelers during inclement weather."

"You might want to take Mom up on her offer," Vanessa said. "She's a fantastic cook. And fast. She has to be with us four kids starving all the time."

Catherine smiled. "With a recommendation like that, I guess I'll have to say yes. Usually Katie, our housekeeper, cooks for us, but she went home sick." She shrugged. "I was going to heat a can of soup and make grilled cheese sandwiches."

Sofia rose to her feet. "Is it all right if I scout around and see what you have?" She was eager to do something. The fire was nice, but she could only sit still for so long.

Catherine waved a hand. "Please, go ahead. If there's anything you can't find or something you need, let me know. I'm going upstairs to check on the guest room beds. I think they have clean sheets, but I want to make sure."

Vanessa jumped up. "I'll come help."

Sofia sent her daughter a grateful smile. She really was a wonderful young lady.

In the kitchen, Julie was just finishing up with Mark. "Give the girls a kiss for me. Love you."

"How's the family?" Sofia asked as she opened the refrigerator door. The enormous space was chock-full of food, including bins of vegetables, exotic cheeses, condiments, low-fat dairy, and—yes!—a big package of organic chicken breasts.

Julie leaned back against the counter, arms crossed. "They're fine. Mark was just getting ready to pick up the girls from dance. Then they're going to hunker down with pizza and a movie. He said the roads are getting worse by the minute." Sofia carried the chicken to the sink to unwrap it. "What are you doing?"

"Raiding the fridge," Sofia said, before pausing for Julie's incredulous eye roll. "Actually, I'm doing dinner for everyone as a thank-you to Catherine."

"Lucky us," Julie said. "What are you making?"

Sofia rummaged through the cabinets for a platter to hold the chicken. "I'm thinking chicken breasts braised with mushrooms, creamy garlic mashed potatoes, and asparagus."

"Perfect!" was Julie's first reaction. Then, "Fresh asparagus?"

Sofia turned on the sink and washed her hands. "Yes, there is some in the fridge. I don't even want to know how much it cost this time of year, but I'll happily cook it."

The lights flickered again as the wind rose to a howling shriek. "Oh my," Julie said. "This is turning into a blizzard."

If it was a blizzard, Sofia was thankful they hadn't attempted to drive home.

She was looking for a large skillet inside a cupboard when a thundering crash shook the house and the lights went out. She jumped, and Julie screamed. As she looked around the dark kitchen, she saw that only the large picture window provided a glimmer of gray light.

"What was that?" Sofia hoped something hadn't fallen on the house.

After what seemed like an eternity there in the dark, Gil appeared in the kitchen doorway, holding a camping lantern in his hand. "A tree came down and took out the lines."

Julie groaned. "I guess we'll be eating a cold dinner."

Sofia found a box of matches on the back of the six-burner gas stove and lit one. To her relief, when she turned the knob, the flame caught. "No, I can cook as long as the gas holds out."

"We have a full tank of propane, so we should be all set," Gil said. He set his lantern on the counter near Sofia. "I'm going to light some more lanterns and candles."

Julie started peeling potatoes and placed them in water to boil while Sofia browned the chicken in oil. Mushrooms and garlic went into the pan to sauté and soften after she removed the chicken. Then Julie moved on to prepare vegetables and dip.

Vanessa popped through the kitchen door. "Yum. Something smells good." She wandered over to the stove to peer at the food. "Did you hear that tree come down?"

"Sure did," Julie said with a chuckle. "Didn't you hear me scream?" She poked a fork into the boiling potatoes to see how they were doing.

"We had to make the beds in the dark," Vanessa said. "You're with me, Mom, in a room with twin beds. Julie gets a queen all to herself." She grabbed a celery stick from the platter of vegetables and dip Julie had prepared.

"Why don't you take that into the other room?" Sofia said. "I'm sure everyone is getting hungry."

Vanessa laughed. "You're right. Richard and Melanie are sitting out there talking about roasting hot dogs over the fire."

"That was my second option," Sofia said, only half joking. Without a gas stove, they might well have been reduced to a campfire meal. She pictured the elegant Melanie roasting a hot dog and smiled to herself.

Catherine entered the kitchen as Vanessa scooted out. "Are you all set in here?" At their nods, she added, "I was just about to open a bottle of wine. Would you like some?"

Sofia and Julie looked at each other. "Yes," they said in unison, then laughed.

The older woman opened a white vintage and poured them each a glass. She glanced at the stove, at the skillet of bubbling chicken and the pan of steaming asparagus. "Everything looks wonderful."

"It will be ready in just a few minutes. Where do you want to eat?"

"How about in here?" Catherine nodded toward the long trestle table under the windows. She picked up two glasses of wine. "After I deliver these, I'll come back and help set the table."

Sofia waved her away. "Don't bother. We have it under control." She found it easier to cook without a client watching her every move.

Once dinner was served, silence reigned over the little group as they tucked into the hot meal. Gil joined them, and Sofia wondered if he usually did, since someone mentioned he lived in an apartment over the garage.

"I tell you what," Richard said. "This meal is the only thing making this situation bearable. It seems like every time I come up here, we lose power. Even in the summer."

"What do you expect?" Melanie rolled her eyes. "We're in the middle of the boondocks. I'm surprised that they even brought electricity all the way up here."

A sarcastic retort about indoor plumbing came to mind, but Sofia suppressed it. Some visitors to Vermont made a point of expressing amazement that the rural area had the same amenities as the city. Instead, she asked Richard, "Where do you live?"

"Boston," was the pithy answer, delivered in a Massachusetts accent. He slid his eyes toward Gil to gauge his reaction to this mimicry.

The other man kept his eyes on his plate as he shoveled in food. "I guess that battery backup on the security system is going to get a workout. I won't be able to get that tree cut and moved until tomorrow." He picked up a bottle of beer and took a swig.

"And they won't make it out here to fix the lines tonight anyway," Catherine said. She glanced toward the window, where the storm still howled. "Who could blame them?"

"I'm sure the power is out everywhere," Julie said. "What a mess."

"I bet school will be canceled." Vanessa grinned.

Richard chuckled. "I always liked snow days when I was a kid. I used to pray for them. Especially when my homework wasn't done or we had a test."

"Exactly," Vanessa said with a smile. She shot a glance at her mother. "Of course, I'm always on top of my work."

"Of course," Sofia agreed. She glanced around the table. "Who wants dessert? I figure we might as well eat the ice cream that's in the freezer with hot fudge sauce."

"None for me, thanks." Melanie stood, smoothing her sweater over slim hips. "I'm going to head to my room and get under the covers before the temperature in here drops to fifty."

"Great meal." Gil set his fork and knife neatly across his plate. "But no dessert for me. I'm going out to walk the perimeter." He drained his beer, then scraped back his chair and left the kitchen.

"Walk the perimeter!" Richard mimicked, his face twisted in mockery. "I'll have ice cream," he said to Sofia. "There's something delightfully irrational about eating ice cream in the winter."

"Yeah, like drinking hot coffee in summer," Vanessa said.

Richard pointed his forefinger at Vanessa. "Exactly." His tone perfectly matched hers earlier.

Maybe Richard is humoring Vanessa. Either that or he's on her level, which is a scary thought.

The rest of the group enjoyed dessert and decaf coffee made in a French press, and then everyone went their separate ways. Catherine loaned them flannel pajamas for the night and provided toothbrushes and toothpaste.

Sofia and Vanessa said good night to Julie, and then climbed into their beds with shivers and groans, thankful for the thick down duvets.

"I feel like an Eskimo," Vanessa said.

"You might want to sleep with that over your head. It's going to get cold in here without heat."

"Gosh, Mom, who would have thought going to a catering meeting would be such an adventure?" Vanessa pulled the covers over her head, her face peering out from a circle of comforter, and said a final good night.

Sofia lay awake for a long time. She always had trouble sleeping the first night in a strange bed. In this case, there was also the discomfort of being stranded and the concern about when they were going to be able to leave. She pictured the snow heaped so high that they had to tunnel out.

The scene outside the big windows didn't allay her fears. The wind howled and heavy snow continued to fall. At times, ice ticked the glass.

There was a long-standing belief that native Alaskans had multiple words for snow, but she had heard that the Scandinavian Sami people actually had more—almost two hundred. All she knew was that as a Vermont native, she had seen them all. Large lacy flakes. Small driving pellets. Flakes that zipped to the ground. Others that drifted, upward even . . . Sofia drifted off to sleep finally, counting snowflakes instead of sheep.

In the wee hours, a different sound penetrated through the

storm. Sofia half awoke. *What was that?* It sounded like a motor whine. She hoped the electric company had come to fix the lines. A little later, the sound buzzed again, and she recognized the noise—snowmobiles. It sounded as if one or more went around the house. So someone was out and about, perhaps driving across the frozen lake. Maybe the came down the snow-clogged road and needed a place to turn around. Perhaps the snow had stopped.

Sofia was too tired to pull back the covers and check. She fell into the strange, dream-filled slumber of morning hours.

Until a scream ripped her out of her fitful doze.

6

The Yorkshire Moors,
April 1850

$\mathcal{B}$eatrice bolted upright in bed as the baby continued to cry. Wasn't anyone going to comfort the child? She waited in the dark, irresolute, then threw back the covers. Maybe no one else could hear the wailing, though why a small infant was sleeping away from a loving parent or nurse was beyond her.

Moonlight streamed through the open windows, and when she glanced outside, she saw that the mist had cleared. The sea was even closer than she had realized, the grounds ending after a short garden enclosed by a wall. Or so it appeared from her vantage point.

Still slightly woozy from being awakened, Beatrice lit the bedside lamp and carried it out into the corridor. Lines of closed doors extended into the darkness in both directions.

The baby fell silent before she could discern which direction the sound had come from. She eyed the door of her room, thinking of her warm bed. But what if the infant needed someone? She wouldn't be able to sleep without knowing for certain that the child was all right.

Hoping she wouldn't stumble into Lord Blackwell's chamber by accident, she went to the first door on her side of the corridor and pushed down on the bar handle, holding her breath. The door swept open silently to reveal another bedroom, heavy furniture looming out of the dark like sleeping creatures.

She pulled the door shut and went to the next, her unease growing as she prowled the dead-quiet hallway. Within the thick walls of the castle, she couldn't hear the sea's assault on the shore. Heavy curtains covering most of the windows increased her sense of isolation and gloom.

By the time she reached the last room in her wing, adjacent to the main staircase, her sense of futility was full blown and she felt rather foolish. The baby's cries must have been a dream. Or perhaps the wind howling in the chimney created the eerie wailing.

Hoping no one had witnessed her creeping about the corridors, she flew back to her room and jumped into bed. Morning twilight cast its first illumination through the window. The horizon revealed a band of light between sullen water and sky. She could hear the first birds starting to chirp outside. With a sigh of relief, she snuggled under the covers and closed her eyes.

"Good morning, miss." Sarah, the housekeeper, bustled into Beatrice's bedroom and set a tray at the bedside with a clatter of china. "I've got tea and toast, but if you want more than that, you'll have to come down to breakfast." She kept her eyes averted, and although her tone was polite, it was distinctly frosty.

Were all guests unwelcome, or was it Beatrice's mission that aroused the woman's distaste? "Tea and toast are fine, thank you. I rarely eat breakfast." Pushing herself to a seated position, Beatrice poured a cup of steaming tea, the amber liquid fragrant. The sun had fully risen, she noted with pleasure, the rays glinting off the waves like chips of gold.

Sarah wiped her hands over her apron. "If that's all, miss . . ."

"I think so." Beatrice added milk to her tea and stirred. "There is one thing I want to ask you, though."

The housekeeper paused at the doorway. "Yes, miss?"

"I heard a baby crying last night."

Sarah's shoulders jerked, and an odd series of expressions flitted over her face. "Are you sure?"

No, I'm not. Beatrice squared her own shoulders. "I thought I did, anyway. But I couldn't find a baby anywhere. Not in this wing, at least."

Sarah turned and trudged toward the bed, her hands wrapped up in her apron as if for comfort. "There is a legend about a crying baby in this house, a sound heard on nights when the mist rises."

An involuntary smile twisted Beatrice's lips. "You mean a ghost? Surely not."

The housekeeper's nod was portentous. "All these ancient houses have ghosts. Why not? They've seen near a thousand years of life and death."

Beatrice couldn't hold back a laugh. "I'm sure there are stories. But honestly, I know what I heard." If the woman had said it was the wind in the chimney, Beatrice would have been content. The woman's insistence that the sound had an otherworldly origin was the purest superstition.

Sarah stopped so close to the bed that Beatrice could see the fine lines bracketing her mouth and eyes. "I'm sorry you heard it, Miss Kimble. They say that bad luck comes to those who do."

Beatrice threw back the covers. "The only bad luck I foresee is making my client wait." Her glance fell on the trunk. "And please send Ettie up to take care of my unpacking. Thank you, Sarah."

Dressed in a dark gray bombazine, the lavender shawl around her shoulders, Beatrice made her way through a maze of rooms to the salon, where the paintings hung. As was her practice, she carried a leather-bound notebook and pencil to take down her thoughts about the collection.

Lord Blackwell and Joseph had arrived first and were standing near the doorway, chatting. "Ah, there you are, Miss Kimble." Blackwell greeted her with a slight bow and a smile. In the daylight, Beatrice confirmed her impression of his attractive features and her sense that he was a troubled man. His smile didn't quite vanquish the shadow in his eyes.

"Good morning, gentlemen." Beatrice eagerly glanced around the salon, glad to see that the vast room faced north and all the paintings were placed away from direct light. In her work, she often found paintings covered with soot and grime or dried out and faded from direct sun. The pigments used in ancient paintings were surprisingly resistant to the ravages of time, but they couldn't withstand abuse or neglect.

"Well, shall we do the tour?" Blackwell gestured with his arms. "After you."

"I trust you had a peaceful night?" Joseph asked.

Beatrice looked over at Joseph to study his face, certain she had heard an undercurrent of malice in his tone. But his expression was studiously bland, his eyes blank of everything but apparent courtesy.

"It was fine, thank you. How about you?"

Before Joseph could respond, Blackwell stopped in front of a portrait of a rather stern gentleman. With relief, Beatrice focused her attention on the piece. That, at least, was understandable and not subject to ploys and maneuvers.

Everything in the collection—sketches, paintings, and an altar triptych featuring the Crucifixion—was rare and valuable.

Lord Blackwell's grandfather had had excellent and refined taste. Beatrice said as much while she jotted notes and impressions. Joseph didn't write down anything; instead, he lagged behind, making occasional remarks under his breath.

"I quite agree with your assessment of Grandfather's judgment," Blackwell said. "If it wasn't for another passion of mine, I wouldn't part with them."

Before Beatrice could ask him what he meant, he led them to the collection's highlight, *Madonna in the Garden* by Renaissance legend Vittore Biagio. Biagio, who had studied under Leonardo da Vinci and Sandro Botticelli, had produced very few pieces. The ones that survived displayed exceeding skill, but that wasn't the whole picture. Somehow he captured a luminosity of light that created a deep response in the viewer.

At least, that was what Beatrice had read. Now she experienced it for herself. The large painting depicted Mary holding the infant Jesus, as so many Madonna paintings did. But this one was set in a lush garden of flowers and fruit, animals peeping here and there through the undergrowth. The central figures glowed, radiating love and peace and joy. Beatrice could feel the young mother's concern for and adoration of her child and his contentment at snuggling safely in her tender arms.

A visceral pang pierced her heart, a flashing memory of her own mother, lost so many years before. Startled, she gasped.

Mortified, she fanned herself with the notebook. "I'm sorry. That wasn't very professional of me. It's just . . ." How could she ever explain?

Blackwell's eyes were sympathetic. "Don't worry about it. Most people react that way. There's something special about it, how it makes Mary and the Christ child so very human."

Even the flippant Joseph appeared affected. "It is a stunning piece indeed." Beatrice heard him whisper something else under his breath, but she couldn't quite hear the words.

"Well, there you have it," Blackwell said. "My collection."

Beatrice turned her back on the painting so she could concentrate. "Where would you like us to work?" She gestured at the table and chairs in the center of the room. "In here?" Their tasks included cataloging the artwork and verifying the provenance through documents in Blackwell's files. In addition, they would examine the works to detect any sign of forgery. More than one collector had tried to pass off a copy as an original.

"In here will be fine," Blackwell said. "I'll have one of the men bring in the boxes of paperwork."

"I agree—this is the best place." Joseph pulled out his pocket watch. "I'll join you later, Beatrice. I have some pressing correspondence to attend to."

Beatrice drew out one of the chairs and sat. "I'll get started on my notes then." Then she thought of Blackwell's earlier remark. "Tell me, what is the passion that is driving you to sell this fabulous collection?"

Blackwell braced his hands on the top of a chair. "I want to start a boarding school for poor but deserving boys, and that requires funding." He grimaced ruefully. "Funding I don't have otherwise."

Beatrice regarded him with surprise. She hadn't expected him to have a charitable heart, which spoke to her presumptions regarding a nobleman's priorities and interests. Despite her admiration, she found herself blurting, "For boys? Girls aren't worthy of an education, then?"

Blackwell's cheeks reddened. "I didn't say that, Miss Kimble. Obviously they are just as intelligent as boys, if your abilities are anything to go by, but—"

"Forgive me, Lord Blackwell. I spoke out of turn." She felt her cheeks heat up at her rudeness. "It's just I'm a little sensitive about the issue." She glanced toward the doorway, praying Joseph was well out of earshot. "I've suffered opposition from most of my male colleagues due to my gender."

Lord Blackwell pulled out a chair and joined her at the table. "I must confess I was surprised when Mr. Kimble told me you would be the lead contact on the assignment. But he assured me that you were most competent and that I was fortunate to have you."

The heat in Beatrice's cheeks turned into a flame. She ducked her head. "How kind of him to say that. I will do my best."

"I have no doubt."

A piercing whistle came from the doorway, and they both turned to look. A small boy dressed in clean but faded trousers, jacket, and cap stood there, grinning. "Who's the lady?"

Blackwell gave the cheeky child a mock scowl. "Mind your manners, Levi. Come and be introduced properly."

The urchin ran into the room, stopping short in front of Beatrice. He swept his cap off his head and bowed low. "Levi Watson at your service, milady."

Beatrice couldn't hold back her laughter. "I'm pleased to meet you, Mr. Watson. I'm Miss Beatrice Kimble, from London."

Levi's eyes were saucers. "London? Where Oliver Twist lives?"

"That's right." Beatrice exchanged a smile with Blackwell, impressed that the young boy had read—or had heard someone read—Dickens. "I'm an orphan too, like Oliver."

The boy gave a hoot of amazement. "Really?" He leaned closer, confidentially. "Did you have to work for an undertaker too? Or pickpockets?" He patted his trousers in the pocket area.

"No, I was lucky to be adopted. My guardian gave me his name and trained me in his profession. I appraise works of art."

Levi gazed around the room. "I like art." He pointed to the Madonna. "Especially that one."

"You have good taste, Mr. Watson."

"Levi, why don't you go to the kitchen and ask Cook for something to eat?" Blackwell suggested.

With a mumbled goodbye, the boy darted off.

"What a bright child," Beatrice said. "Is he one of your future students?"

Blackwell nodded. "He's an orphan, and I've taken him under my wing. He comes up here most days to do extra lessons with me."

No wonder Levi was fascinated with Oliver Twist and other orphans. "Where does he live?"

"With his uncle, who is a fisherman and a nice chap, but he and his wife have ten other children. So Levi gets lost in the shuffle."

Ten! Beatrice pictured them all clamoring for their mother's attention. No wonder Levi preferred coming to the castle. "I can understand that. He's lucky to have you."

He shifted his shoulders as if to shrug off her praise. With a tap of both hands on the table, he stood. "Lunch is in an hour. Do you think you can find the dining room if I leave you here?"

"I think so. Please, be about your business. I'll just finish up some preliminary notes."

After a light meal attended only by Blackwell and herself, Beatrice wrote a letter to Horatio to let him know they had arrived safely and work was underway. She didn't mention the attempted robbery or the fact that her partner had apparently disappeared.

It wouldn't be very professional to report Joseph's behavior to Horatio, although she was sorely tempted to complain. As lead appraiser on the project, it was up to her to make sure he did his share, not go missing and flit around the countryside. She would have to give him a dressing-down, a task she dreaded, once he resurfaced. Confrontation wasn't natural to her, no matter how hotly she seethed inside.

Beatrice signed her name, folded the letter, and sealed it with wax. The afternoon was lovely, and she thought to walk down to the post office. If Joseph could take a holiday, so could she.

Levi joined her on the walk down to the village, promising to show her the way. The path took them along the cliff top, a narrow track worn deep by decades of foot traffic.

"You can take the road if you like, Miss Kimble," Levi said. "But this is much shorter."

"And much prettier." Beatrice paused to gaze at the ocean, calm and gently rippling under a tender blue sky. Sea birds wheeled and dipped over the waves far below, and she glimpsed a crescent of sandy beach between rocky headlands. Spring scents of dirt and green growing things mingled with the salt air. "Is it possible to go down to the beach?"

"On that path." Levi pointed to two boulders guarding the way down. "But you have to be careful not to get caught down there when the tide comes in." His large eyes were earnest. "But if you go down there at low tide, there are caves."

"Caves? Tell me about them." Beatrice began to walk again, enjoying the boy's company as he went into a discourse about the caves that apparently riddled the cliffs.

"But if you see the light on the headland, don't go to the caves." He dropped his voice to a whisper. "It's dangerous."

"And why is that?" Beatrice thought she could guess what he was talking about. Smugglers probably used the caves to store goods and used the light as a signal for all others to stay away.

"I don't know. But you shouldn't. Promise not to?"

"I promise." She had no plans to tangle with smugglers. A group of highwaymen had been enough.

The path began to dip downward, and they entered a copse of woods. Then the path curved toward the sea again, and the village of Castlerock appeared—houses and a church clinging to the abrupt slopes of the small harbor. They left the path and stepped onto a cobblestone street.

"Where's the post office, Levi?"

He pointed to a house down by the harbor, stone like all the rest but with red shutters. "There's a store there too." He smiled at her, a hopeful look in his eyes.

"Would you like a sweet for helping me today?"

"Oh yes, miss, I would." He began to skip downhill so fast that she had to call to him to slow down.

The street took them past the docks, a busy area where men unloaded boats, repaired nets, and gathered in pairs and groups to discuss business. Strong, tangy odors of fish and seaweed hung in the air, and gulls wheeled and cried above in their endless quest for food. A faded sign lettered The Black Dog and illustrated with a rendition of the legendary barghest identified a dingy building as a public house. Men sauntered in and out, greeting one another, smoking pipes, and cursing robustly. Some of them were worse for wear, and she quickened her steps, not wanting to be accosted by an overly friendly sailor.

Then she saw a familiar figure striding toward the pub, as out of place in the setting as roses in a ditch in his fine tweeds. While she watched, he flung open the heavy pub door and disappeared inside. What on earth was Joseph Norris doing down here at the docks?

7

Cabot Falls, Vermont,
Present Day

"What's going on, Mom?" Vanessa's head popped out from beneath her comforter.

Sofia threw back her own covers, heedless of the bone-chilling cold. "Someone screamed. I'm going to find out what happened." Locating a small woolen throw on a chair, she draped it around her shoulders for warmth. At least the storm had ended and the sun was out, glowing through the frost feathers on the windows.

The bedroom door opened, and Julie stuck her head in. "Did you hear that?" She, too, wore a blanket, draped over her head and held close to her cheeks.

"Yes. Let's go." Sofia scurried out of the room and down the gallery hallway to the stairs. Peering over the railing, she saw the great room was empty, although a fire roared in the fireplace.

Julie was on her heels. "Where did it come from, do you think?"

Before Sofia could speculate, Catherine appeared in the doorway of the jewelry room. By the dazed expression on the woman's face, Sofia guessed something terrible must have happened to Catherine's precious collection. Sofia ran the rest of the way down the stairs, holding the bannister so her stockinged feet wouldn't slip. "Catherine, what's going on?"

The woman sagged as Sofia reached her side. "They're gone. The best pieces are gone."

Sofia put her arm around Catherine so she wouldn't fall and, with Julie on the other side, gently guided Catherine to the sofa. Once she was safely settled, they hurried into the jewelry room. Although the room was lit only by daylight streaming through the doorway, Sofia could tell the cases were mostly empty, the pieces Catherine had said were most valuable plucked like fruit from a tree.

Julie gasped. "How did this happen?"

"I'd like to know that too." In a haze of disbelief and shock, Sofia wandered through the room, noting all the empty spaces. The diamond brooches were gone, as were most of the millefiori.

"Did the security system go out because of the power?"

Sofia shook her head. "Gil said there was a battery backup. Or else what would be the sense? Anyone could cut the wire and you'd be vulnerable." She ran her hand through her hair, thinking. That noise last night . . . snowmobiles.

"You're right. That would be quite a coincidence. How would the thief know the power was out?" Julie followed Sofia back out to the living room and the welcoming warmth of the crackling fire.

"Catherine, did you hear anything last night?" Sofia asked, perching on the sofa beside the distressed woman.

Catherine shook her head. "Not a thing." Her cheeks flushed as she plucked at a velour afghan draped over the sofa back. "I often take . . . um, sleeping aids, you see, and they knock me out." Her eyes brightened with hope. "Did you hear something? Did you hear the thieves?"

"I'm not sure. I did hear snowmobiles going by in the wee hours. At one point it sounded like they circled the house. Of course, it could have been anyone. You must get a lot of snow-mobilers out here at the lake."

The older woman sagged in disappointment. "Yes we do. Although it wasn't very good snowmobiling weather last night."

"I wonder how anyone got out here during the storm," Julie said. "The roads were terrible."

"That's true," Sofia said. "They're probably still not plowed."

As if in response to their conversation, the roar of a motor and the familiar thump and scrape of a plow sounded from the front of the house.

"Is someone here to plow us out?" Sofia asked.

"That's Gil. We keep an old truck around for plowing."

What if the thieves weren't on snowmobiles? Gil could be destroying evidence by plowing the driveway. "Excuse me a minute." She hurried for her boots and coat. "I'll be right back."

Despite the sunshine, the air was brisk, like a cold slap on her cheeks. Ducking her head against the wind, Sofia trotted up the driveway toward the pickup truck heading her way, pushing a wing of snow. She might be too late.

She waved her hands, and Gil pulled to a stop beside her, rolling down the window. To protect against the weather, he wore an insulated canvas jacket, heavy leather gloves, and a cap with earflaps. His nose and cheeks were red with cold.

"What's up?" he asked, obviously impatient to keep working.

"There's been a robbery. Most of the jewelry is gone."

He frowned. "You're kidding."

"No. I wish I were. Someone got in during the night and wiped out most of the collection."

He stared straight ahead, chewing on his bottom lip. "That blasted alarm. I knew it wasn't going to work, even with a battery backup."

Sofia hid her annoyance at this shifting of blame to the Halls. "That's up to the police to figure out. The reason I came out is to stop you plowing. You may be destroying evidence."

"Evidence?" His heavy brows beetled in another frown.

Sofia pointed at the pristine drifts of snow. "Tracks. Tire, footprints, snowmobile." She shrugged. "Cross-country skis, even."

"I didn't see any tracks. The main road isn't plowed yet, so they must have come in another way."

She'd have to take his word for it, she realized. Most of the driveway was now rutted with the truck's treads or scraped clean by the plow. "I'll let you get back to work. I'm sure the police will appreciate a clear driveway."

"Tell Catherine I'll get after that tree next," he called after her. The culprit in question was a birch, broken off at the trunk and lying across the side yard where the electrical wires came in. A little closer and it would have hit the garage roof.

Sofia stamped the snow off her boots on the porch steps and went inside. As she was unzipping her coat, she realized she should check the back of the house for tracks. Otherwise, Gil would tramp around and spoil them. She waddled through the great room, rezipping her coat as she moved toward the back of the house.

"Where are you going, Sofia?" Julie asked, stopping on her way into the kitchen. "I'm going to put a kettle on for coffee."

"I just want to check something out back. I'll be right back." Unlatching the sliding door, she stepped out onto the back porch. Beyond the covered portion, the open deck was buried in snow. Sofia waded through the snowdrifts, annoyed when quantities of wet fluff slid into her boots but determined to test her snowmobile theory. To make the situation even more uncomfortable, snow kept blowing off the roof and hitting her in the face. But she merely squinted and pressed on.

At the edge of the deck, something made her glance up at the second floor, where she spotted Vanessa staring down at her. She waved at her daughter, who made a comical and questioning gesture at seeing her mother outside. Sofia smiled and kept moving toward the railing.

Her effort was rewarded. In the backyard, quite close to the house, snowmobile tracks were pressed as clearly into the new snow as railroad tracks across a field. *That's how the thieves managed to get here while the roads were shut down.* In addition, law enforcement was otherwise engaged with accidents and other emergency transport situations. Seemingly a perfect crime.

Sofia gratefully reentered the semiwarm house to find Julie making coffee and Vanessa sitting by the fire, playing with her phone. "Mom, we've got to get a signal somehow and call the police. I can't even get one bar right now."

"I agree. We should call the police. As soon as possible," Sofia said. "The snowmobiles I heard came right up to the house, so I think that's how the thieves got here."

Vanessa threw her an admiring look. "Awesome. I wondered what you were doing out there."

"Thanks for your help, Sofia." Catherine sat huddled in the corner of the sofa, hands between her knees, her shoulders shaking in shock. "I have no idea what to do first."

Sofia took a seat next to her, grabbed the velour afghan, and draped it around Catherine's shoulders. "Julie is making hot drinks. That will help."

"Thank you," Catherine said again, gathering the blanket closer. She raised her head and looked at Vanessa. "If you go upstairs on the deck outside my room, you might get a signal. It's worked before."

Vanessa jumped to her feet. "I'll try."

"Call the police and tell them there was a robbery," Sofia said. "And mention that we don't have power and need to be plowed out. The road, I mean. The driveway is clear. Oh, and give Dad a call to let him know we're okay. Ask him to call Mark for Julie."

"Okay, Mom. Wish me luck."

"Where is everyone else?" Sofia asked Catherine after Vanessa bounded up the stairs. She was surprised Richard and Melanie hadn't heard Catherine scream. A dark suspicion twanged. Were they still at the house, or had they run off with the jewelry?

Julie bustled into the room, carrying a tray of coffee mugs. The fragrance was ambrosia to Sofia's nose.

"Richard and Melanie sleep in the other wing upstairs." Catherine waved her hand in the direction of their bedrooms.

"I was wondering where the rest of the crew was." Julie handed around the mugs. "Probably huddled under the covers."

Sofia sipped at her coffee. Attempting to sound nonchalant, she set the cup on the table and stood. "I'm going to check on Richard and Melanie, tell them breakfast is coming. Scrambled eggs sound good, Catherine?"

"Fine. Not that I can eat anything. But please, help yourself."

"I'll be back down in a minute." Sofia padded across the room and headed upstairs, her heart beating faster. What if Richard and Melanie were the thieves? That would be a simple solution. Or Gil? Maybe his helpful handyman routine was a ruse.

Vanessa came scampering along the upstairs hall. "I finally got a signal, Mom. The police are on their way." Shivering, she rubbed her arms. "I sure hope they bring the power company with them. I'm freezing. I got through to Dad too."

"We're having breakfast soon. Maybe that will help warm you up." Sofia pointed to a door she assumed led to the other wing. "I'm going to check on the others, make sure they didn't freeze to death overnight."

Vanessa scooted for the stairs, still clasping her phone. "I'm going to get as close to that fire as I can. Maybe crawl right in it."

Sofia crept along the short hallway, holding her breath in trepidation. There were four doors, all closed. She knocked on the first. No answer. Feeling like an intruder, she turned the handle and pushed the door slightly open.

A bathroom. Cross off that room. She moved to the next and rapped, a little more loudly this time. "What is it?" A female voice. Melanie.

Sofia thought about yelling through the door, but that wouldn't be effective. Hoping the woman wouldn't mind the intrusion, she opened the door and stuck her head in, speaking to the heap of covers on the bed. "Hi, Melanie. I hate to bother you, but someone broke in last night." She paused. "They stole most of Catherine's collection."

The heap shifted and twitched, and Melanie's head appeared. "What?" She brushed her disheveled hair into place and narrowed her eyes. "Are you serious?"

"Very." Sofia kept the information about the snowmobiles to herself. "The police are on their way. We're about to make breakfast downstairs, if you want to join us."

Melanie shoved the covers back and thrust her feet into slippers. "I'll be right there. Does Richard know?"

"Not yet. I was just on my way to tell him." Before Melanie could forestall her, Sofia shut the door and moved along the hall. She wanted to see Richard's reaction to the news for herself.

The door on the end belonged to him, judging by the grunts and groans her knocks elicited. Footsteps thudding across the floor told her he was coming to the door, to her relief; she really didn't want to barge into a strange man's bedroom.

"What is it?" Richard was tying the sash of a ratty blue terry cloth bathrobe around his thick middle. His eyes were bleary, and his greasy hair stood up in a crest. *Not a morning person, apparently.*

She shared the news of the theft, watching his face carefully. To her surprise, he didn't exclaim in shock or anger. Instead, he rubbed his stubbly chin and frowned.

"Did you call the police?" He shook his head. "Of course not. The lines are down." He flicked the light switch next to the door up and down. "Yep. Still out."

"My daughter managed to get a cell phone signal, and the police are on their way." Sofia stepped back out of the doorway. "I'll let you get dressed."

On the way back downstairs, Sofia reflected on the pair's reactions. Melanie was shocked but not overly so. Sofia still didn't have a good read on the young woman. She appeared efficient but cold and didn't seem to be especially close to Catherine. Richard seemed mildly concerned rather than upset. Some men were that way, stuffing their emotional reactions in favor of logical problem-solving.

Julie was already in the kitchen, stirring a big pan of eggs with a wooden spoon. "Do you want to take over?" she asked Sofia with a smile.

Sofia peered into the yellow mixture, which included tiny chunks of onion, green pepper, and mushroom. "No, it looks great. Set the heat low, and keep stirring so they don't stick." She opened the bread box. "Oh, good. Blueberry muffins. I was wondering how we were going to toast bread."

"I take it the others were upstairs," Julie said. She lowered her voice. "Do you think they might be involved?"

"I don't know what to think. Why didn't that alarm go off? That's the big question." Sofia pulled stoneware plates out of the cupboard and placed them on the counter. "Gil plowed the drive, thank goodness. Maybe we'll get out of here today."

Before Julie could say anything, the sound of a chain saw reverberated from outside. "Gil must be working on the downed tree now. Hopefully we'll get electricity back." Sofia opened the silverware drawer. "After breakfast, I'm going out to take a closer look at those snowmobile tracks. Maybe there will be a clue where they came from." She threw Julie a grin. "Don't worry—I won't mess them up before the police see them."

"I'm coming with you." Julie set her jaw in determination. "Something is really strange about this whole setup."

After a quick breakfast, Sofia and Julie put on their boots and coats, claiming the need for air and the desire to take pictures of the snow-covered lake. Melanie and Richard gave them skeptical looks but seemed disinclined to leave the fireside. Gil had loaded the woodbox, and throwing an occasional log on the flames was the extent of Richard's efforts.

Since the deck steps were filled with snow, they went out the front and walked toward the side of the house, wading through more than a foot of fresh, powdery snow.

Gil stopped the chain saw when he saw them approaching. "Where are you going?" he shouted.

"Just for a short walk," Sofia called. "Get some air."

He shook his head as if to say they were crazy. After they trudged into the deeper snow of the side yard, Sofia thought she might agree with him. In addition to the drifted banks, the ground sloped, making the footing treacherous.

"Whoops!" Julie's arms windmilled as she slipped. With a shout of laughter, she regained her balance. "I should have brought my skis."

"Or a sled." Sofia slid her feet forward slowly, not wanting to fall. Behind the house, the land leveled off, creating a backyard that ended at the water. There was a boathouse with sections of dock stacked beside it and a gazebo in a copse of trees.

"Sofia, I think they must have gotten in that way."

She followed Julie's pointing finger to a door under the deck. From where she stood, she saw that one of the glass panes had been broken. "I think you're right."

Putting a hand to her brow to cut the glare, she searched the sparkling snow for tracks. There they were, about six feet away. She slogged closer, waving for Julie to follow.

The churned-up snow showed where the thieves had stopped. "See, Julie, there was more than one." Two sets of front skis were clearly visible.

"They're facing this way, so they must have come from that direction." Julie thought for a moment. "From the east."

"And they kept going." Sofia noticed that the tracks didn't return in the direction from which they approached but continued to circle the lake.

Julie groaned. "I bet these don't lead right to someone's house. That would be too easy." She gestured at the serene vista of lake and hills. "I bet there are tons of trails around here."

"And there are thousands of snowmobiles too." Sofia's stomach sank. As a clue, the tracks were pretty slight. She bent over and studied the tracks more closely. Was there a chance that snowmobile tracks varied by make and model, like tires? She'd seen forensic shows where they took impressions of tire tracks.

Her pulse leaped when she spotted a difference in one tread. "Julie. See that? One of the machines has a studded tread."

8

The Yorkshire Moors,
April 1850

*B*eatrice stared at the pub door as if it could tell her that she really had seen her colleague entering its seedy shelter.

"What's the matter, miss?" Levi asked, his face screwed up in puzzlement.

"Wait here, Levi. I'll just be a moment." Without stopping to consider her actions, she briskly crossed the street and entered the pub. Whistles and catcalls followed her passage, but she ignored them. It was broad daylight, after all.

Inside, she had to blink her eyes to see anything in the dark pub with its low beamed ceilings and tiny, grimy windows. The air was thick with tobacco smoke, and someone was boiling cabbage. Humped shapes of men lined the bar and sat at small tables. Without exception, they all turned to stare at her, their faces sallow moons in the murk.

Feeling horribly conspicuous, Beatrice scanned the crowd for Joseph. He didn't appear to be there, which was strange. After a moment, seeing that she wasn't going to do anything noteworthy, the men returned to their drinks and conversation.

Beatrice stood there, shifting from foot to foot, irresolute. Should she walk through the room or forget the whole thing? Then she caught the eye of the barmaid, a pretty young woman with high-piled blond hair and a sulky expression. She would ask her.

"Did you see a gentleman wearing tweed come in here?" She gestured. "Tall, with light hair and blue eyes?"

The woman stared at her, mouth gaping, as if she were inquiring if the barghest himself had paid a visit. "I don't think so, mum. Only working folk come in here." Her eyes raked Beatrice up and down as if to say, "Not the likes of you." Her smirk fell on a hulking brute seated on a nearby stool. "Isn't that right, Ned?"

Ned raised his foaming mug in a salute. "If you say so, Dot. Although I might take a wee bit of offense at not being considered a gentleman." He laughed coarsely.

A thrill ran through Beatrice. Had she heard that gravelly voice before? She thought back to the few words the highwayman had said. She couldn't tell for sure, but they sounded similar.

"Away with you, Ned." The barmaid picked up a filthy rag and began to wipe the bar, moving away from Beatrice. "You're not a gentleman, and you know it."

Thus dismissed, Beatrice pushed her way outside, grateful for the relatively fresh air of the docks. Levi was waiting, sitting on a wall and swinging his legs. When he saw her emerge, he jumped down and skipped over. He took her hand, staring up at her with wide eyes. "I'm glad you didn't get your throat cut."

Beatrice glanced over her shoulder at the pub. "Was that a possibility?"

"It's where all the ruffians go." The boy shrugged. "Sometimes they fight."

She shuddered. "Well, you won't catch me in there again, I promise."

In contrast to the pub, the combination post office and grocery was tidy and cheerful, with pansies blooming in the window boxes. Inside, the space was crammed with dry goods, housewares, and bins of fresh produce. At Beatrice's nod, Levi headed for the counter, a penny clutched in his hand, to study jars of treats lined up like a display of riches.

Two middle-aged women ran the place, and by their similar features, Beatrice guessed they were sisters. The one behind the post office window was slightly older, judging by the gray hair under her cotton-print bonnet. All the women in town except the barmaid seemed to wear the style, which featured ruffles along the crown and a quilted edging.

"Help you?" The postmistress seemed to study every detail of Beatrice's appearance. The sign by her window read "Miss Ann True."

"Yes, please." Beatrice slid the letter across the wooden counter, worn smooth over the decades. "Post to London."

Beatrice looked over at the candy counter and saw Levi point to the sweets he wanted—lemon drops and a peppermint stick.

Miss True took the envelope. "New to the area, are you?"

"I'm staying up at the castle."

"The castle, eh? Are you enjoying it then?" Her tone implied she expected the opposite. She weighed the envelope and slapped stamps on it.

"Yes I am, thank you." She forced herself to smile at the woman. Except for Levi and Lord Blackwell, everyone she had encountered so far was remarkably unpleasant.

"So what did you think of Castlerock?" Blackwell asked that night at dinner.

"It seems to be a nice little place," Beatrice said. *Except for the people.*

Again they were seated near the fireside in the dining

room, and in anticipation of the warmth, Beatrice wore her new black lace shawl instead of the wool. She adored its swirling pattern of flowers and leaves and how it draped like gossamer on her shoulders.

"I enjoyed walking down and back with Levi," she went on. "He showed me where the post office is."

"And who is Levi, may I ask?" Joseph asked with a cocked brow as Wesley, the butler, presented a platter of Cornish hens. Joseph pointed to the largest.

Beatrice left it for Blackwell to answer. "Levi is a young boy from the village. He's very bright, and I'm planning to see that he is educated."

Joseph picked up his knife and fork and cut into the hen. "That's good of you. But isn't the village school adequate?"

Blackwell accepted a hen from the butler. "It is, as those things go. The basics are covered. But if students want to go beyond that, there is no option."

"It's very admirable of you to take an interest," Beatrice said, taking a bite of succulent chicken topped with some sort of sweet fruit glaze. *Delicious.* Whatever the castle's shortfalls in comfort, they had an excellent cook. "Lord Blackwell is going to found a school," she told Joseph. She threw the nobleman a teasing glance. "I'm going to talk him into accepting girls as well as boys."

Joseph gave a short laugh. "I pity you, Blackwell. She can be quite relentless."

"Only when circumstances call for it." Beatrice changed the subject, watching her partner carefully. "What did you do this afternoon, Joseph?"

He speared a roasted potato chunk and popped it into his mouth. "Not much. Walked on the moors for a while. Trying to get the feel of the place. Might do some sketching." He smiled smugly. "I've had quite a bit of interest in my nature sketches."

"Is that so?" Blackwell's response was polite. "I'd like to see them when you have time."

Beatrice filed away Joseph's explanation, noting that he hadn't included his trip to The Black Dog. What was that? If it had been an innocent quest for a draught of ale, surely he would mention it. Or was he ashamed of his desire for drink?

"I'm glad we both enjoyed some fresh air today," she said carefully. "But tomorrow we'll need to get to work."

Joseph grimaced, then adjusted his face when he saw her glare. "Of course. How long has Horatio given us? Two weeks, right? Plenty of time."

Although fuming at his flippancy, Beatrice held her tongue. She was thrilled to be put in charge of their project but hadn't anticipated such defiance from her colleague. Gaining his cooperation gracefully without resorting to her guardian's assistance would be a true test of her diplomatic skills.

After dinner, the men retired to the billiards room with port and cigars at Beatrice's insistence. Following Blackwell's directions, Beatrice found her way to the library. At the sight of floor-to-ceiling bookcases crammed with leather-bound volumes, she caught her breath. She could stay a century and never read all these books. Blackwell had explained that they were organized and labeled by subject—history, literature, science, philosophy, and classics in Greek and Latin.

She went right for the literature, hoping to find something entertaining to help her relax. Inspired by Levi, she located a volume of *Oliver Twist* in a group of novels by Dickens. She loved his rich descriptions and characterizations, even if he could be a little wordy. In addition, the story of poor Oliver Twist reminded her most forcibly of how fortunate she was to have been adopted.

Both of her parents had died in a cholera epidemic when she

was only three, far too young to remember much about either of them, unfortunately. She knew only that her father was descended from the great Italian composer Sebastian Ripa. He, too, had been a musician.

With a sigh, she tucked the novel under her arm and continued to browse. Remembering the strange stories she had heard from Sarah and Joseph, she decided to read a book about Yorkshire history and legends. *Forewarned is forearmed, right?* At least no one would catch her off guard with their fantastic tales.

Beatrice took the books upstairs to her room, where the lump-like and seemingly mute Ettie came to help her undress. Beatrice slid into bed, thankful for the low fire burning in the grate. The clear day had given way to indigo night, and a silver half moon was rising out of the sea. The waves were only a faint murmur against the shore. Beatrice left the window open, preferring fresh air and the view despite the chill.

She opened the history book first and learned that Yorkshire had either been settled by the Romans, the Gauls, or the Britons, a matter still of some debate. Apparently Roman ruins and artifacts were often discovered under layers of later settlements. The rest of the book was an odd mishmash of stories about the early saints in Yorkshire and the supernatural legends of hobgoblins, witches, and, of course, the barghest. As was the case in much of rural Britain, the old ways still lingered.

After her head started to nod over the Dickens, she set the book aside and shuttered the lantern. In the middle of plumping her pillows, she heard a sound.

Oh, please. Not the baby again. She held her breath and listened. No, this time it sounded like an adult sobbing, alternating soft wailing and woeful moans. Was one of the servants upset? She thought about ignoring the cries, but compassion won out along with curiosity.

She lit the lantern again, determined not to stumble around in the dark. Out in the hall, she stopped to listen. The sounds seemed to be coming from the central hall where the three wings of the house came together.

Just like the night before, there didn't seem to be another soul in the vast house. Was she the only one who heard the strange noises? Her bare feet on the carpet were silent, her lantern a tiny spot of light in an ocean of black. A gust of cold air made the flame dance.

"Who's there?" she called. "Is something wrong?" Every part of her wanted to run back to the shelter of her room. Was there a lock on the door? She couldn't remember.

The crying continued without pause, leading her to the gallery at the top of the grand staircase. Something white flickered in the moonlight streaming through the tall windows. She had the impression of long skirts, a nightdress perhaps.

"Sarah? Ettie? Is that you?"

No answer. The figure turned and flitted toward the door to the west wing, which was abandoned, according to Sarah. All the public rooms and bedchambers in use were in the east-facing keep or the north and south wings.

The door to the west wing opened silently and the figure entered, moving slowly as if to beckon Beatrice onward. The wails and sobs continued.

She stepped into the corridor, holding her lantern high to get her bearings. The air in the west wing was not only bone-achingly cold, but it also reeked of must and mildew. The walls oozed with damp, darkening the stone. The carpet runner was grimy and dank underfoot. Something dripped somewhere.

Chills ran down her spine. The woman had disappeared.

9

*Cabot Falls, Vermont,
Present Day*

Sofia pulled out her phone and took a picture of the studded snowmobile tread marks, positioning herself so shadows highlighted the divots. "This is a great clue."

"Really? Why's that?" Julie asked.

"Not all snowmobile tracks have studs. One of Jim's friends does, and he has to put them on himself." She stepped into a different position and took another shot.

Engines rumbled and flashing blue lights reflected off the snow-covered trees in front of the house.

"The troops are here," Julie said.

Sofia checked the photos, then tucked her phone into her pocket. "I'm glad they made it. Maybe the roads are improving."

A familiar freckle-faced figure dressed in a thick winter parka and cap with flaps trudged around the corner of the house. Officer Ryan Quimby of the Cabot Falls Police Department. He waved. "Sofia. Julie. What are you doing out here?"

Sofia pointed to the tracks. "I heard snowmobiles last night. I think the thieves used them since the roads were in such bad condition."

Ryan trudged down the slope to where they stood. He regarded the tracks dubiously. "Anyone could have made these. Snowmobilers cruise around out here all the time."

"But they stopped in back of the house, see?" Sofia jabbed her finger at the break in the tracks. "And look at the studded treads."

"Hmm. Quite a few people use those. They work great on ice."

"Really, Officer Quimby, you should get someone to photograph them," Julie put in. "The sun is getting stronger, and soon the tracks will be mush."

Sofia hid a smile at her friend's support of her theory, considering her earlier skepticism.

"Maybe so." Ryan gazed around at the lake and woods. "Anything else you noticed out here?"

Sofia pointed toward the house. "We think they got in through that door."

The officer gazed up at the door below the deck, his brows rising when he spotted the broken windowpane. "You could be right." He spoke into his shoulder microphone attached to the radio on his belt, telling his partner to check the lower entrance. After he finished, he asked, "What are you two doing here, anyway?"

Sofia explained their purpose for visiting Catherine and how they had gotten stranded during the storm.

Ryan appeared to be absorbing the information as he pulled a notepad out of his pocket and began to jot things down. "So you were here during the robbery. You didn't hear anything?"

Sofia shook her head. "No, nothing except the snowmobiles. And Catherine screaming, of course, when she discovered the theft."

"I didn't hear anything. Not even the snowmobiles." Julie mimed pulling blankets over her head. "I was under the covers trying to keep warm. Then the screaming woke me up."

"So the alarm didn't go off?" Ryan asked.

"No, and that is really strange," Sofia said. "David Hall was just here servicing it yesterday afternoon." She didn't mean it as a criticism of David's work, so she was disconcerted when Ryan fastened on that tidbit.

"Really? That is very interesting. A break-in right after the alarm was serviced." Ryan nodded as he tucked away his notebook. "I'll get right on it. Thanks."

An hour later, they were released to go home, although the police were still questioning the members of the household. With great relief, Sofia navigated the Suburban down the driveway and onto the lake road, which fortunately had been plowed and salted. She was dying for a hot shower and fresh clothes. And to see the rest of the family, which went without saying. The radio said school was canceled, and she pictured the children's joy when they learned that good news. They were probably bouncing off the walls.

Julie gave a big sigh. "I feel so terrible for Catherine. What a loss."

"And what a violation." Sofia had suffered break-ins by people interested in her grandmother's quilt, so she could sympathize with the woman's outrage and fear.

In the backseat, Vanessa obviously was playing with her phone. "Darn. I wish I could get a signal."

Sofia glanced at her in the rearview mirror. "Who are you calling?"

"Ethan. I can't believe they think his father had anything to do with the burglary."

Sofia winced. "I don't either, but you really shouldn't say anything to Ethan about the break-in. Or anyone else for that matter. I hate to say this, but it could be construed as interfering with an investigation."

Vanessa's jaw dropped. "Seriously?"

Julie turned to face the teen. "I agree with your mom. I'm sure once they investigate, they'll find out that the Halls had nothing to do with it."

"I hope so. But the whole thing stinks." Vanessa reluctantly tucked away her phone. "And we're all out of a job because of it too."

Sofia realized Vanessa was right. No need now for the catering or the public relations campaign. "I'm disappointed too, honey. But there will be other opportunities."

"That's right, Vanessa," Julie said. "I'll find another project for you."

"Thanks. I really appreciate that. But I have to say, her jewelry was really cool."

It certainly was. And extremely valuable to boot. Although Sofia believed that whoever rode the snowmobiles was responsible for the heist, she had a feeling there was more to the story. In her view, the break-in was an inside job and David Hall was merely the fall guy.

After a stressful ride over slippery roads, they finally pulled into Sofia's cul-de-sac. At the Parker house, the three younger children, bundled in snow pants, jackets, hats, and mittens, were shoveling the walk and front steps, assisted by Fergus gamboling through the piles of snow.

When Matthew saw the trio climb out of the SUV, he threw down his shovel and ran over, followed by the others. "Mom! You made it." He threw his arms around her waist. She squeezed him back, joy rising in her chest as it always did when she was reunited with her family, no matter how short the time they were apart.

Vanessa laughed. "Of course we did, silly. We were just stranded, not lost."

"I'm glad you guys are home," Wynter said, her face solemn. "The power went out, but it just came back on."

"I heard they canceled school," Sofia said. "I thought they might, what with all of the snow."

Matthew pumped a fist. "Snow days rock."

"If the power's back, that means we have hot water," Vanessa said. "I'm taking a shower ASAP." She scurried for the door.

Jim appeared in the doorway after Vanessa passed, a big grin on his face. "The travelers return. I've got coffee brewing."

"Thanks, Jim." Sofia sighed. "That sounds perfect."

"I'll take a cup." Julie glanced at her phone. "Then I'd better get home, check on Mark and the twins."

"We brushed off your car," Luke said. "Look." He pointed proudly to Julie's snow-free car parked in front of the garage.

"Thanks, Luke. That's really nice of you." Julie gathered her tote. "I'll just put this in my car, then I'll join you inside."

"Can we take a break, Dad?" Matthew asked. "I'm cold." He shivered in an exaggerated fashion. "I think I need hot chocolate."

Jim and Sofia exchanged amused glances. "All right," Jim said. "But then you have to finish."

As Sofia was carrying her own things toward the house, she heard a sharp bark and a hail of greeting. Her elderly next-door neighbor, Pat Cooper, was walking her poodle, Willow, along the street. Pat's husband, Homer, was a former art history professor, and Pat had been an English teacher at Cabot Falls High. Pat wore a down coat, fur-lined boots, and a wool hat topped by a big pompom. To Sofia's amusement, Willow was also dressed for the weather in a red sweater adorned with about a dozen white pompoms.

"How did you and Homer make out during the storm?" Sofia asked. "I hope you stayed warm."

Pat huffed slightly after trotting up Sofia's driveway. "We were fine, thanks to our pellet stove. I'm so glad we put it in last year."

"That's good to hear." Sofia shifted her tote to her other hand. She was dying to join everyone inside for coffee and then jump into the shower after Julie went home. But she didn't want to be rude to her friend, so she silently prayed she wouldn't linger long.

"I heard you had to spend the night out at Lake Lucy," Pat said. "The kids told me."

"That's right, we did. At Catherine Stanley's house."

Pat's eyes went wide behind her glasses. "The place that was burgled?"

"How did you hear about that?" News certainly did travel fast in Cabot Falls.

The older woman smiled smugly. "I didn't tell you? Homer bought me a police scanner for Christmas." She leaned closer and whispered, "Let me know if you want me to help you crack the case." A big fan of television crime shows, Pat relished the opportunity to assist with any real-life mystery, no matter how small.

"Oh, Pat, that's up to the police."

"They always seem to need our help," Pat pointed out. "And I bet they will with this case too." She sighed enviously. "You are so lucky to have been there."

Sofia laughed. "That's not how I'd put it, but you're right, it was interesting." A thought struck her. Pat seemed to know everyone in the area. "Say, do you know Catherine Stanley or any of the people who live with her?" Sofia told Pat the names of the people from the Stanley household.

Pat didn't know Catherine, Richard, Melanie, or Gil, although she had heard about the tragic death of Catherine's husband. But she was acquainted with the cook and housekeeper. "Katie Smith is the one to talk to, even if she was home sick last night. Her mother taught science at the state university before she became ill. Brilliant woman." Pat tapped the side of her head. "Katie's a chip off the old block. She'll know who's on the up and up. Or not."

"I'm glad we did this," Julie said as she entered the Parker house again that evening. "I was starting to feel snowbound with the twins home all day. They finally left for a sleepover."

"Tell me about it," Sofia said with a laugh, taking the wine bottle her friend handed her. "My crew had a bad case of cabin fever. Thank goodness it's Family Friday at the bowling alley. Jim took the three younger kids and Marla's Tim. And Vanessa went to the movies with Ethan."

"Any news on that front? With David Hall, I mean?" Julie unwound her scarf and took off her coat.

Sofia shook her head. "All I know is they were questioning both of them this afternoon." A car door slammed outside. "That must be Marla."

A soft knock on the back door announced the arrival of the third member of the Pinot Painters, Marla Dixon. She was dressed for the weather in a pale blue parka trimmed with faux fur that set off her wavy blond hair and blue eyes. "Hi, guys. I heard you had quite an adventure last night." She set down her easel and tote and began to remove her coat and boots.

"We sure did," Julie said. "We'll tell you all about it." She moved to the counter and lifted the lid of a slow cooker, releasing a mouthwatering aroma. "What's this, Sofia?"

"Chicken cacciatore. Nonna's recipe. While you open that wine you brought, I'll dish us some." Sofia nudged her friend out of the way and picked up a serving spoon.

"Aye-aye, kitchen boss." Julie saluted with a smile, then began to twist a corkscrew into the cork.

"Thanks for feeding us this evening," Marla said. "What a treat."

"This is one of my favorites on a winter night." Sofia filled pottery bowls with chunky chicken, mushrooms, peppers, and onions swimming in a rich tomato sauce. "Marla, can you pull the garlic bread out of the oven?"

"Gladly." Marla grabbed an oven mitt and opened the oven door, fishing out the foil-wrapped loaf. "Oh, did I tell you? I wrote to a contact at the National Gallery in England. He's going to see what he can find out about Beatrice Kimble. I also brought some reference books about lace to compare with the quilt."

"That's great. Thank you." In the excitement of the previous twenty-four hours, Sofia hadn't given much thought to the quilt and her ancestor, aside from a quick call to Marla after her shower. She wouldn't have thought of it at all if she hadn't had to change into clean clothes and spotted the trunk. It was nice to turn her mind, however briefly, from the growing knot of dread she carried concerning David Hall. Earlier that afternoon, she'd realized that even if they didn't pin him to the robbery, they might discover negligence or incompetence in the installation of the security system. That wouldn't do his business any good. Catherine might even have grounds to sue if he had made a critical error that resulted in thieves gaining access.

Julie filled three wineglasses and placed one at each place setting. "You know, Beatrice might have worn jewelry similar to the pieces that were stolen. They were from the same period."

So much for that hiatus. Even talking about my ancestor provides a reminder of the situation. "I had the same thought." Sofia gestured for the others to take a seat. "That collection was truly spectacular."

Marla picked up her spoon, pausing it over her bowl. "Tell me what happened. I'm dying to hear all about it."

Sofia and Julie filled Marla in while they ate, Julie describing the preparation for the auction and their involvement while Sofia added her observations about the house's residents.

"I was shocked to wake up to the news of the theft," Sofia said. "I can't believe such a major crime happened in that tranquil spot. During a snowstorm no less."

"What's even more tragic is that Catherine was donating the auction proceeds to charity," Julie said. "She's got to be one of the most generous people I know."

"Catherine funded the children's wing, right?" Marla said. "I haven't met her, but I do know her housekeeper, Katie Smith. She checks out a stack of books every week."

"Pat Cooper knows her too. She told me Katie's mother was a brilliant science professor at the state university," Sofia said. Although there was nothing wrong with being a housekeeper, she did wonder why the apparently intelligent Katie hadn't followed in her mother's footsteps.

"Brilliant, huh?" Marla raised her brows. "That's high praise from Pat. She's a tough old bird, especially in the classroom." They all laughed, having experienced the rigors of having Mrs. Cooper drill them in proper English grammar and usage.

"Every time I write a proposal or a press release, I think of Pat," Julie said. "She sure taught me how to string sentences together."

"I love teachers like her," Marla said. "Sometimes I think literacy is in grave danger from the use of texting shorthand and slang."

"I'm cutting back on the girls' screen time," Julie said, "and making them read actual books."

"Good idea." Marla beamed. She scraped her spoon along the inside of her bowl with a sigh. "That was a fabulous meal, Sofia."

"I'm glad you liked it." Sofia pushed back her chair and stood. "Ready to paint?"

After helping Sofia clear, they adjourned to the four-season room off the kitchen and set up their easels. Sofia loaded another couple of logs into the woodstove, dislodging the napping Fergus to do so, and then they got to work.

Inspired by Lake Lucy, Sofia worked on a landscape depicting a round lake tucked under snowcapped peaks and surrounded by evergreens. She was well into the work, accompanied by the crackling of logs and the dog's gentle snores, when the phone rang.

Sofia rose from her easel to pick up the receiver in the kitchen. It was Vanessa, crying so hard that Sofia had to wait with a pounding heart until her daughter became coherent.

"Mom, the police are considering Ethan's dad a suspect in the robbery."

10

The Yorkshire Moors,
April 1850

Beatrice raised the lantern with a trembling hand to extend its reach, unable to believe the woman had actually disappeared into thin air. But the golden shaft of light revealed only an empty corridor lined with closed doors. Heart hammering in her chest, she crept along, both fearing and hoping to see the wraithlike figure again.

She reached a stairwell, the wide steps descending into a deep, inky void. Had the woman gone down the stairs? She studied the risers, noting the thick dust covering the stone. She hadn't come this way, then. A cold draft rose from the lower story, curling around her bare ankles and touching the back of her neck like a ghostly caress.

As the silence of the deserted wing deepened, her desire to escape welled up in a rush of panic. With a strangled sob, she turned and ran down the corridor, intent only on getting back to her room.

Once safely inside, she set down the lantern and locked the door using the brass key she found on the mantel. Then she searched the room in a frenzy—under the bed, in the wardrobe, even behind the draperies. Nothing and no one. Gulping in deep breaths, she stood, hands on hips, allowing the rhythmic roar of the surf to soothe the shocks of fear still tingling in her limbs.

Before getting into bed, she fluffed the pillows. As she lifted one, a small black object about the size of a large coin flew off the bed and onto the floor. Curious, she picked it up and held it to the light. A rough oval made of shiny black stone, it was carved with a woman's face surrounded by tangled hair. Peering closer, she saw the strands were snakes.

It was the head of Medusa, from ancient mythology. That rang a bell concerning something she had recently read. She set the stone on the bed and picked up the book of Yorkshire legends sitting on the bedside table, thumbing through to the section on Roman inhabitation of the area. *Ah, there it is.* The minor gemstone jet was used to make jewelry in Roman times and was regarded to have magical properties protecting the wearer from the evil eye.

She set the book aside and picked up the stone, letting it rest in her palm. *An amulet against the evil eye.* Almost without thinking, she threw the unholy thing into the corner of the room. Who had left it in her bed? And why?

Pounding on her door woke her to another day of sunlight streaming through the open windows, the dancing bay beyond.

Knocking sounded again. "Miss Kimble? Are you all right?" It was Sarah's voice.

A huge yawn stretching her jaws, Beatrice sat up and pushed back the covers. After a couple of wakeful hours pondering the unsettling events of the night, she had finally fallen into a deep, dreamless sleep.

"I'm coming," she called, shuffling to the door and turning the key.

"I'm sorry, miss." A disheveled Sarah picked the breakfast tray off the floor and bustled in. "You didn't answer my first knocks, and when I realized the door was locked, I got worried."

Beatrice yawned again. "I'm sorry, I was fast asleep." Perching on the bed, she watched the woman pour a cup of tea, then thanked Sarah with a nod and a smile as the housekeeper handed it to her. There was nothing like the first sip of tea in the morning to clear one's head.

Sarah smoothed her apron with both hands. "Is there anything else I can get you, miss?"

Beatrice considered mentioning the crying woman but decided it was fruitless. The last thing she needed was another warning of doom. Her eyes flickered to the piece of jet lying on the rug in the corner, and she shuddered. The same with that thing. Obviously someone was trying to scare her, since she doubted it was a kind gesture that led someone to put it in her bed.

She wouldn't give them the satisfaction of letting them know she noticed or was concerned, she decided. She pasted a wide smile on her face. "There is one thing, Sarah."

"Yes, miss?" Sarah's eyes were eager as they darted about the room. Looking for the amulet, perhaps?

"Please inform Mr. Norris that I will meet him in the gallery in one hour sharp." She set her cup in the saucer with a clatter. "We have a lot to do today."

Sarah's face fell, as did her eyes, which examined the polished brown boots peeping from under her serge dress. "Yes, miss. I'll tell him."

"Thank you." Beatrice picked up a piece of toast and took a crunchy bite, hiding her satisfaction. She would keep her door locked, she decided, and refuse to investigate any more crying or screams. That would put a stop to the fun and games.

As Lord Blackwell promised, the boxes of correspondence and

paperwork were on the gallery table when Beatrice swept into the room exactly one hour later. To her satisfaction, her associate was also there, although she didn't approve of the slovenly way he was leaning back in a chair and paring his fingernails with a knife.

"Joseph!" she said, her tone sharp. "What are you doing?"

The front legs of the chair thumped down. "Waiting for you." Seemingly unruffled by her rebuke, he folded the knife and tucked it into his pocket. He gestured at the row of boxes and ledgers. "Shall we begin? Apparently we have to sift through this lot for the information we need." His curled lip told her what he thought of that.

"That is a chore." Some clients provided neatly packaged lists and files detailing their collections. Apparently Blackwell's grandfather wasn't one of them.

Taking a seat, Beatrice thought for a moment about how best to proceed. Their task had three components. First, they needed to identify and authenticate the works in the collection. Then they needed to review provenance, the chain of custody of ownership. That helped eliminate stolen or forged works—most of the time. The final step was to determine a value for the pieces, individually and collectively. Others at the gallery would review their work before a final offer was made to Blackwell.

To complicate matters, some of the work was unsigned, and additional research was needed to decide upon an approximate period and associated value.

"You can either catalog or start digging through the paper-work," Beatrice said. "Your choice."

Joseph pulled a coin from his pocket. "Let's toss for it. I call heads."

Beatrice delightedly won the flip and chose for herself the task of taking the inventory. That involved studying each piece at length and making notes and sketches. A few of the pieces were by artists with other known works, which would help date the pieces as well as provide information for comparison. While she worked, she remained conscious of the serene Madonna, and she couldn't resist stealing frequent peeks at the compelling painting.

"How are you getting on with everything?" Blackwell appeared in the doorway at noon. "Lunch is ready, if you'd like to take a break."

Joseph threw down the file he was studying with a grumble. "Sounds good to me. This is quite a—" He stopped abruptly when Beatrice darted a glare in his direction.

"We're doing very well, Lord Blackwell." Beatrice tucked a strand of hair into place, hoping she didn't have smudges on her face from the sketching pencil. "But this is a perfect time to take a recess." She laughed. "I can only absorb so much at one time." She set down her things and moved toward the doorway. "Just give me a few minutes to wash up, and I'll join you."

She thought she heard Joseph mutter something about the size of women's brains, but she resolutely turned her back and marched out of the room. All morning, he had sighed and moaned while sorting through the papers. It was most distracting and unprofessional to boot. She had half a mind to write to her guardian to have Joseph removed from the project.

Lunch was lamb stew and freshly baked bread with an assortment of local cheeses on the side. Beatrice found the veined blue cheese to be an especially good spread on the bread.

Blackwell gave a sigh of satisfaction as he set his spoon neatly beside his empty bowl. "What are your plans for the afternoon?"

Before Beatrice could answer, Joseph said, "I'd like to stretch my legs, take a ramble. Maybe do some sketching."

Beatrice glanced at the windows overlooking the side garden. The sunlight of the morning had disappeared, eclipsed by glowering clouds threatening rain. Wind tossed the trees and bushes, tendrils of mist winding through their branches.

"It's not exactly a good day for a stroll on the moors," she said. "I was thinking we would press on. There is a lot to do."

"Come now, don't be such a slave driver." Joseph's tone was light, but the glare he sent her was challenging. "We can do another session after tea. I work better if I have a chance to clear my head."

"By all means, clear your head," Beatrice said. "Perhaps that will smooth your progress through the paperwork." Her words were calculated to provide a mild reproach.

Apparently they hit their mark, for Joseph dropped his eyes, cheeks flushing.

Blackwell cleared his throat, and Beatrice guessed by the glint of humor in his dark eyes that he'd heard the subtext in their words. "Would either of you care for dessert or coffee?" At their headshakes, he'd told the butler, "We're finished. Thank you, Wesley."

Joseph hustled from the room, Blackwell and Beatrice following more sedately. In the doorway, Blackwell reached out a detaining hand. "If you are free, Miss Kimble, would you like a tour of my proposed school? I plan to set it up in the west wing, and I could use a second opinion about some things."

The west wing! Beatrice felt a thrill of excitement at the thought of exploring it in daylight. Perhaps she could figure out where the mysterious woman had gone.

"I'd love to accompany you, Lord Blackwell," she said. "It would be an honor. Give me half an hour?"

Blackwell's smile was warm. "Meet me in the great hall. We'll go from there."

"You can see the place needs a lot of work," Blackwell said with a laugh. He and Beatrice stood in the main reception hall in the west wing, a sizable chamber with stone walls, flagstone floors, and a beamed ceiling darkened with centuries of woodsmoke from the cavernous fireplace at one end. Tattered wall tapestries and a heavy trestle table with benches were the only furnishings.

Beatrice took a step across the room, holding her skirts away from the thick dust that coated every surface. With a sense of pleasure, she noted the arched windows, the carved columns, and the graceful sweep of the wide staircase. "The proportions are pleasing, though. I can see how grand this room once was."

Hands clasped behind his back, Blackwell gazed around ruefully. "After the keep, it is the second-oldest part of the castle. Once my great-grandfather came into his whaling fortune and built the north and south wings, most of it was abandoned."

Beatrice turned, taking in every detail. "This will be the assembly hall for the students, I suppose?" If she used her imagination, she could picture lines of eager pupils standing to be addressed by their headmaster.

"That's what I was thinking." He sauntered to the fireplace hearth. "I will lead them in prayers every morning, accompanied by an improving thought for the day."

Beatrice joined him at the fireside, running her hand along the carved stone mantel. "How fortunate they will be, those boys . . . and girls perhaps?"

His brow creased. "You aren't giving up on your promotion of a coeducational school, I see."

"I never give up when I know I am right." She gave him a cheeky grin, and to her relief, he laughed.

He rolled his eyes in mock patience. "Well, make your case, then."

"Have you heard of the Dollar Institution in Scotland? It is a day and boarding school that serves the local poor but attracts wealthy pupils with its excellent education. They specialize in helping each student succeed by developing their unique talents and abilities."

"And you believe that I can provide such an education to my pupils?"

She flushed at her own presumption, wracking her brain for how best to answer. Truly it was his tender manner toward the orphan Levi that inspired her belief that he was a deeply caring and capable man. But such an admission felt too intimate for their slight acquaintance.

"After I saw the size and depth of your library, I was convinced you could." She paused. "And upon considering the magnitude of your sacrifice in selling your splendid art collection, I knew you would."

To her surprise, his expression became somber. He ducked his head. "Ah, Miss Kimble, you flatter me. It isn't nobility of soul that drives me, but rather a realization of my own need for atonement."

Beatrice thought of Joseph's poisonous words in the coach on the way to the castle about the death of Blackwell's wife. *Does he feel responsible?*

An uneasy silence stretched out, becoming almost unbearable. Then he visibly shook himself. "Pardon me. I have much on my mind, and I'm being rather a bore."

"Not at all. Do you have more to show me?" She seized upon a topic. "How will you feed the pupils? From your own excellent kitchen?"

"Thank you for saying so; I do have a wonderful cook. But as a practical matter, we would need to prepare meals for the students in this wing." He pointed at a nearby door. "The kitchen and storerooms are through here, but they're in even worse condition than the rest of the rooms." He grimaced. "There was a fire in the kitchen recently, and no one has touched it since."

"An expensive undertaking, then, to repair that area?"

"Yes, but not horrendously so. Fortunately the structure is still intact. The damage was mostly from the smoke."

Beatrice reached for the latch. "May I?"

"It's filthy in there, not fit—"

"I don't mind. I enjoy exploring." She pressed the latch, which was surprisingly easy to open, and pushed the door open. A rush of cold, dank air blew into her face, and she thought she detected an underlying odor of soot. From the fire, no doubt.

The hallway was narrow, lined by yawning doors leading to the storerooms, which looked like empty, toothless mouths. A thin beam of sallow daylight from over her shoulder provided the only illumination, but Beatrice could clearly see something odd. The flagstones weren't uniformly dusty; in fact, the center of the floor was almost free of dust. Someone—or multiple someones—had walked through here recently. The lady in white, perhaps?

Then she saw something else even more peculiar, something that made her jump and cry out.

A man's face loomed out of the dark, the lit candle he held illuminating his hooked nose and fiendish, snaggletoothed grin.

11

Cabot Falls, Vermont,
Present Day

"Can you repeat that, Vanessa?" Sofia wasn't sure she had heard her daughter's tear-filled words correctly. The connection wasn't great either.

"I said, Ethan's dad is definitely a suspect. The police asked him to come to the station for questioning. Ethan said they had to call a lawyer." Other voices spoke in the background, and Vanessa took her mouth away from the phone. "I'm talking to my mom. She'll be able to help."

Sofia hoped Vanessa's faith was justified. When Vanessa came back on, she asked, "What grounds did the police have, do you know?"

Again Vanessa consulted someone. "They said it was something to do with the security system. They can prove it was tampered with."

Sofia's heart sank. That wasn't good, unless someone else who lived at the house or had access to it had sabotaged the system. She took a deep breath. "Vanessa, tell Ethan not to worry. We have a friend who can help."

Vanessa's voice was much brighter. "Thanks, Mom. You're the best. We're going over to Ethan's to keep his mom company, but I'll be home before curfew."

"Take your time, hon. I know it's rough for them." After she hung up, she turned to face her friends, who were agog. She quickly filled them in, and both of them expressed dismay and concern.

"Who is the friend you mentioned?" Julie asked.

"I can guess," Marla said, her cheeks pinking. "Thor Anderson, right?" Marla sometimes dated the former Army Intelligence expert, a good friend of Jim's.

"That's right," Sofia said. "If anyone can crack the problem with the security system, it's Thor. He's got his own private investigation firm now."

"I remember Thor. He sounds like a great person to bring in," Julie said. "What else can we do? Now that they're blaming David, I guess we'd better get involved."

"You're probably right." Sofia began to pace around, trying to work off her anxiety. "I think someone who lives there is involved. But how can we find out more? Since the project is cancelled, we don't have a reason to visit Catherine."

"Someone should talk to Katie Smith," Marla said. "Maybe she'll spill the beans about Catherine and company. If there are any to spill, that is."

"Someone?" Julie cocked a brow. "But who?"

Marla and Sofia looked at each other. "Pat Cooper," they said in unison.

"I'm thrilled you want to include me in your investigation," Pat whispered to Sofia. She shifted the container of chicken soup she held to the other arm and rang the bell. They were standing on the porch of Katie Smith's house, a small but nice white frame house in an older Cabot Falls neighborhood. According to Pat, Katie had inherited the house from her parents.

"Katie being sick gave us a great excuse." Sofia smiled. "Being nosy about her boss might not have gone over so well."

They heard the sound of footsteps, and Pat gave Sofia a wink in response. "We're on." She adjusted her expression to a neutral smile of neighborly good will.

The door opened, revealing a stocky woman in her midforties dressed in gray sweatpants and matching top. Her attractive face was bare of makeup, and her dirty blond hair was disheveled. She gave a wan smile when she recognized Pat. "Mrs. Cooper. How nice to see you." She ran a hand over her hair, trying to straighten it. "Excuse my appearance. I'm just getting over the flu."

"So I heard from my neighbor Sofia Parker." She nodded at Sofia. "Catherine Stanley told her you were sick." Pat brandished the container. "I thought I'd bring you some of my famous chicken soup." She put one foot on the threshold, gently insistent upon entering.

"And I have a dozen fresh-baked rolls to go with the soup," Sofia said, indicating her tote.

"How kind of you both. Please, come in." Katie stood back to let them inside the house.

Sofia first noticed a pleasant odor of lemon wood polish. They stood in a small, square, wallpapered hallway, a staircase rising to the right. A doorway on the left led to a living room furnished with overstuffed chintz and a braided rug; the one on the right, to a dining room. Interestingly, the table held books, reams of paper, and a laptop.

"Katie writes romantic suspense novels," Pat told Sofia as they followed the other woman to the kitchen. "She publishes them under a pen name."

"Shh. That's my secret," Katie said. She gestured to the red Formica-and-metal table. "Have a seat. I'll put on the kettle for tea. Unless you'd rather have coffee?"

Sofia and Pat agreed tea was fine. The kitchen had the same friendly, old-fashioned feel as the rest of the house. The appliances were older but spotless, and the counter was also Formica instead of the ubiquitous granite everyone else had.

"Taking a few days off from work, I hope?" Pat asked.

"I had to." Katie opened a tall cupboard and pulled out three mugs and a teapot. "I haven't been that sick in years."

"I'm glad you're feeling better," Sofia said. She pulled out the rolls and set the bag on the table. "Heat these at 350 degrees for ten minutes and you'll be good to go."

"Thanks." Katie picked up the rolls and carried them to the chrome bread box. "Yum. Did you make those?" She moved to the stove after stowing the bread just as the kettle began to whistle.

"Yes," Pat said before Sofia could speak. "In fact, she was supposed to cater Catherine's auction."

Katie paused in the action of filling the teapot with boiling water. "Really? So you know about the robbery, then."

Sofia felt a spurt of relief at how easily the subject had been broached. "I sure do. I was there that night. My friend and I were stranded in the storm, along with my daughter."

The other woman finished pouring the hot water and put the lid back on the teapot, setting it on the table. "We'll let this steep a minute." She sat in the chair between Pat and Sofia, her head going back and forth as she spoke. "So, tell me what happened. Catherine called me, of course, but I'd like to get your take."

Sofia told her the sequence of events in detail, while Katie poured tea and let them doctor theirs with milk and sugar. "I feel just terrible about it," Sofia concluded. "The collection was spectacular, and Catherine was so generous to donate it to charity."

"And now they're blaming David." Katie's mug thumped down on the table. "What a crock."

"You know David Hall?" Sofia asked.

"Of course I do. We were in the same class in high school. His wife was—and is—a good friend."

"They were both my students," Pat said.

Katie patted the former teacher on the shoulder. "Like everyone else in town, Mrs. Cooper. We're all victims—er, *grateful recipients* of your instruction."

Sofia hid a smile at this gentle teasing.

Pat shook her finger at Katie in mock anger. "Now, now. I've told you more than once. Call me Pat. We're both of age."

"All right. Pat." Katie winced. "That hurt, but I suppose I'll get used to it." They all shared a laugh.

Sofia brought the conversation back around to the crime. "If you think David is innocent, which I do too, of course, who could have done it?"

"Hmm." Katie picked up her mug and took a sip while she thought. "This is just speculation, you understand, but her son didn't want her to hold the auction." She shook her head. "Unfortunately I overheard a few fights over it."

Pat tsked. "That must have been unpleasant."

"Richard didn't want her to sell." Sofia pondered this information. "But would he steal from his own mother?"

"I hate to think so," Katie said. "But you never know. They aren't exactly close."

"Even though she lost her other son?" Sofia felt a pang of grief in sympathy for Catherine. She couldn't imagine such a loss.

"She had another child?" Pat raised her brows in surprise. "I didn't know that."

"Richard had a twin," Katie said. "He died at birth. Which makes it all the more tragic that they don't get along. I gathered from things Catherine said that Richard's always been a handful, especially after his father died when he was a preteen."

Sofia pictured a rebellious Richard, her mind absurdly painting a picture of his balding head on a younger body. She hadn't especially warmed to him, but it was the other two she really wondered about. "What do you think of Gil and Melanie?"

Katie snorted. "Melanie's got her eye on Richard for his inheritance, but good luck to her pinning down that slippery fish. And Gil?" Her face went a little dreamy. "There's something odd about him. He seems way too sophisticated and skilled to take a position as handyman and chauffeur."

"I could say the same thing about you," Pat pointed out. "You were one of my best students."

Katie's laugh was rueful. "Yeah, I know. But I stayed here to take care of my parents. And I like working for Catherine. It's easy and pays well and gives me time to work on my novels."

"Maybe Gil is a closet writer too," Sofia quipped.

"If so, then he's writing an espionage novel. He's as cagey as a spy." Katie gave a decisive nod. "I'll bet the thieves had inside help."

"I agree," Sofia said. "Now we just need to prove it."

That evening, Sofia served up homemade sausage-and-pork meatballs and spaghetti to a full house. The dinner list had mushroomed to include Pat and Homer, Marla and her son, Julie and her family, the Halls, and Thor Anderson.

"Good thing I tripled the recipe." Sofia ladled sauce onto the bowls of spaghetti Julie held out to her while Marla ran servings into the dining room, where the other adults were enjoying glasses of wine. The younger kids had already been served in the kitchen; the older ones would join the adults.

"It's good practice for catering," Jim said, laughing as he pulled loaves of garlic bread out of the oven. He quirked a brow at the kids, who were goofing around and making lots of noise. "If you can handle this bunch, the sky's the limit."

"No kidding." Vanessa turned her attention from the huge vat of salad she was serving into small bowls. "Quit blowing bubbles in your milk, Matthew."

The exuberant Matthew was even more animated than usual with Ellie and Cindy Butler and Tim Dixon as an audience. Luke, in contrast, shyly ignored the girls, who were his age, but loudly told Tim a series of foolish jokes, making the other boy hoot with laughter.

"Hard to believe we used to act like that," Ethan Hall said. He picked up two pitchers of homemade salad dressing. "Where do these go?"

"One in the dining room and one in here," Sofia said. She glanced around. "I think we're all ready. Does everyone have salad, Wynter?"

"Yes," Wynter said, coming back into the kitchen.

Jim handed Wynter the baskets of garlic bread. "Put these out, and I'll say grace."

Everyone tucked into the meal with gratitude, and even the kids were quiet for a while.

"Thanks again for having us over," Bonnie Hall said. She was a short, pleasantly plump woman with a brown bob and a huge smile very like her handsome son's. "It's been a terrible week. We appreciate the support." According to the Halls, David hadn't been formally charged, but their attorney said it didn't look good. Although he had an alibi for the night of the burglary, the police thought he rigged the system to allow the thieves entry.

"Of course we support you," Sofia said. "We know David is innocent."

Her friends all murmured agreement.

"We're going to help you prove it," Jim said. "That's why my good friend is here." He clapped Thor, clad in a black turtleneck, on his broad back. Thor Anderson, with his hawklike features and blond crew cut, always wore black.

"Really?" Bonnie's eyes were wide. "I thought you were up from Boston for a ski vacation, Thor."

Thor gave a rumbling chuckle. "I was. Then Jim tapped me with this situation. How could I say no? Obviously the unsub tampered with the security system without leaving fingerprints, or so I assume, based on the police team's report." He shrugged one muscular shoulder. "Of course, their work is not without flaw."

The others were staring at Thor in amazement. Correctly interpreting their expressions, Jim said, "Thor is former Army Intelligence."

"I was in the Army," Homer said. "Served in Korea as a medic."

Thor acknowledged the older man's contribution with a brief salute. "Always good to meet a fellow serviceman."

"What does *unsub* mean?" Bonnie's eyes were wide with confusion.

"Unknown subject, of course," Pat said. Her tone was crisp, as if to imply everyone should know that. "What do you do now?" Pat asked Thor. "Homer became a professor after he was discharged." She patted her husband fondly on his knee. "Taught history at the local college for thirty years."

"Nothing so intellectual. I'm a security consultant." Dimples winked when Thor flashed a grin, an effect similar to the sun briefly touching a glacier. Marla, who sat on Thor's other side, could barely tear her eyes from the man's chiseled face.

"Obviously your knowledge is a little more sophisticated than mine," David said. "Although I installed a state-of-the-art system in the Stanley house."

"You put one in our house, and it's worked great," Mark Butler said. A mechanical engineer, Mark had a calm and deliberate manner that complemented Julie's vivacious personality.

"That's right, it has," Julie added. "We haven't had a single problem."

"You do good work, Dad," Ethan said, rising to bolster his father's defense. "What we installed for the Stanleys was the latest and best stuff. We even checked it the day of the break-in."

"Unfortunately, criminals make a habit of deconstructing systems as fast as they are designed," Thor said. "Whoever is involved in this robbery appears to be an expert."

"We think it's an inside job," Pat said. "Right, Sofia?"

All eyes turned to Sofia. "It's a strong possibility," she said. "I heard snowmobiles come by and stop in back of the house, but I have a hard time believing someone who was unfamiliar with the house would be able to disarm the system without some kind of knowledge."

"Snowmobiles." Thor rubbed his square chin. "Good choice under the weather conditions."

"And hard to trace," Mark said. "There are hundreds if not thousands of snowmobiles around here." He shook his head. "How can we check every registration?"

"We have evidence," Julie sang out. "Sofia noticed that one of the snowmobiles was using studs, and she took pictures of the tracks. Are studs common?"

"The state allows them, but they're like putting nails on your treads," David said. "Studs can rip up the roads, and people don't like doing that."

"Yeah, my friend who uses them only drives that snowmobile on ice," Jim said. "He doesn't go on asphalt at all."

"That might narrow it down some," Thor said. "You took pictures?" he asked, turning to Sofia. He gave her a thumbs-up. "Good move."

"I did." Sofia scurried to the kitchen for her cell phone, checking on the kids while she was there. They were busy eating and weren't making too much of a mess, she noticed gladly. Back in the dining room, she scrolled to the best photo and handed the phone to Thor, who glanced at it before passing it around the table.

"There will be a lot of snowmobiles at the Winter Carnival," Bonnie said. "David and I were in the races last year."

"Yeah, your team won your class." Ethan's smile was proud.

"The old fogey class," Bonnie said with a laugh.

Jim snapped his fingers. "That's right, they have an ice race."

"And every year someone tries to sneak in studs," David said. "They're not allowed."

The phone had come around to Sofia's hand again when it rang. "It's Catherine Stanley," she said.

"Go ahead, take it," Julie urged. "We don't mind."

Everyone at the table fell silent, waiting for Sofia to conclude the short call.

"I'll get back to you right away, I promise," Sofia said. "Hang in there." She disconnected. "You won't believe this." Sofia looked around the table, her heart pounding. "She just got a ransom demand for the collection. One million dollars."

12

The Yorkshire Moors,
April 1850

*B*eatrice's eyes fluttered open. The first thing she saw was Blackwell's face, a concerned look in his eyes. She struggled to move, only to find herself constrained by the lord's arms. She gasped.

"It's all right, Miss Kimble. You fainted. I had to catch you."

Fainted? She could scarcely believe it. She wasn't the type to get the vapors like other foolish females. Of course, her sleep had been interrupted two nights in a row. She was exhausted. That must be it.

Blackwell went on. "If you're all right, I'll set you down."

"Yes, please." Her voice was a squeak. How mortifying to be handled so by her client!

Blackwell set her down, and Beatrice felt the flagstones cold and unyielding under her hips and legs, rapidly clearing the lingering haze in her mind. She leaned on one hand to further steady herself, heedless of the grit under her palm.

"I saw a man in the hallway." With her other hand, she pointed to the open doorway. "He was horrible looking. And he smiled at me." She shivered. "An evil smile."

Blackwell frowned and shook his head. "A man? I didn't see anyone."

He was still beside her, and whenever he moved, she got a

whiff of the bay rum he used as scent, her favorite on men. Her treacherous nerves betrayed her with a rush of pleasure.

With an effort, she turned her mind back to the issue at hand. "He had a hooked nose and a rather large chin." She demonstrated the man's features on her own face. "Go see for yourself."

He put both hands on his knees and rose, then strode to the doorway, disappearing down the hallway. Within a moment or two, he returned. "I didn't see anyone."

"There was someone there. Didn't you notice that the flagstones don't have any dust?" Her voice was triumphant. She tucked her feet under her and stood, assisted by Blackwell. Her legs were still wobbly, and she was forced to allow him to steady her.

With an arm around her shoulders, he guided her to one of the benches at the trestle table. "Have a seat. You are obviously still not well."

Biting her lip, she accepted his help once again. "Take a look for yourself. Everything in here is covered with dust. But that hallway isn't." A thought struck her. "Where does it lead?"

He crossed his arms and regarded her with mingled amusement and annoyance. "You are set on this notion that you saw someone, aren't you?"

She stiffened her spine. "I am. Maybe I am just an imaginative female, but my eyes work quite well." She batted her lashes with exaggeration. "Humor me, please. Is there access to the kitchen from other parts of the castle?"

Blackwell sighed. "Yes. One exit leads to the cellars. There is also a servant's staircase for access to the upper stories."

That fit. She would bet anything that the ghostly woman escaped down the back stairs. She studied Blackwell's impassive face. Should she confide in him, or rather confront him about her eerie experiences? *Why not?* she decided. Perhaps then these strange visitations would cease and she could get a full night's sleep.

"The man is not the only strange visitor to this wing."

His head jerked. "Whatever do you mean?"

She described the wailing woman and the cries of the infant that had disturbed her during the previous two nights. Training her eyes on his face, she watched him closely for a reaction. "Your housekeeper told me that hearing the baby was a sign of bad luck," she concluded.

His face had displayed a succession of emotions—surprise, concern, then disdain. "I'm afraid you must have had unusually vivid dreams, Miss Kimble. Unlike other Yorkshire castles, I can assure you that this one is not haunted, no matter what nonsense the servants prattle."

Stung by his unjust remark, she sprang to her feet, thankful to realize she was fully recovered from her earlier weakness. "How dare you! Your servant is the one who told me the legend—after I heard the infant's cries, not before."

"She probably took advantage of your dream to tease you. I'll speak to her, if you wish."

"Don't bother. I'll put cotton in my ears tonight to block any untoward sounds. The ghosts can have full run of the place for all I care." With this sharp remark, Beatrice turned on her heel and marched out of the room. Once back in the great hall, she paused, noticing to her dismay that her knees were shaking once again. She didn't know what had upset her more, the strange visions or the fact that Blackwell didn't believe her. Then an even worse thought struck: *What if he is behind the events?* Why, she couldn't imagine, unless it was a plot to keep people from inquiring too deeply about his affairs. With a sick feeling in her belly, she remembered Joseph's insinuations about Blackwell's business activities.

She would need to be sure that the provenance and authenticity of the works was impeccable. Otherwise, the gallery might make an ill-advised purchase that would hurt the institution's finances and reputation. As well as her own career and that of her guardian.

If Blackwell was innocent, then her thoughts were entirely unworthy, and she hoped he would never suspect her doubts. That was the problem with hearsay and rumor; they tainted everything.

Back in the main castle, she decided to go to the gallery to continue working. Her jumbled thoughts and unsettled emotions required some sort of discipline, and she knew from experience that absorbing tasks were the best thing to clear one's mind.

To her surprise, Joseph joined her, the cuffs of his pants still damp from tramping on the moors. Without saying much, he sat down and began to pore over a thick, dusty ledger. They worked in silence for a while, the only sounds the crackling of the fire and the hushed footsteps of the butler on the carpet as he came to add a log or two and check on their needs.

Around five o'clock, Blackwell appeared in the doorway, dressed in his traveling cloak and hat. "I have to leave for a day or so on urgent business," he said without preamble. "I just received a message about something I must address immediately."

Beatrice noticed with a sinking heart that he refused to meet her gaze. Was he angry at her bluntness? She always seemed to regret it when she spoke frankly to a man. They hardly ever responded well.

"Don't let my absence stop you from continuing the appraisal," Blackwell went on. "I'm sure you're as eager as I am to bring this business to a conclusion."

"We're always glad to spend the gallery's money," Joseph said, grinning to take the edge off his words. "Aren't we, Beatrice?"

Why did he have to drag her into his ill-mannered rudeness? "We are always happy to acquire fine works, he means." Beatrice smiled at Blackwell, but he still refused to look at her. "Have a safe journey, then, and we'll see you soon."

Blackwell gave a curt nod and, with a mutter of farewell, left with a swirl of his cloak. Once his footfalls faded, Joseph stretched his arms overhead, fingers laced.

"Ah. At last he is gone." His grin twisted into a smirk. "Now I can tell you what I've learned." He slapped the open ledger with his hand. "I can't find any information about the late Lord Blackwell's purchase of the Madonna painting."

Cold dread trickled through Beatrice's veins. This news meant disaster. If Blackwell had obtained the painting illicitly . . . She wrested her mind from that terrible thought and gestured at the paperwork spread out over the table. "There must be something in there somewhere."

Joseph hoisted his feet onto the table, crossing them at the ankles and leaning back in his chair, hands behind his head. He was the perfect illustration of arrogant insolence. "You're welcome to look."

"I will. Because I don't believe you." Frantically, she pulled the nearest file toward her and began to riffle through it. He must be lying, probably trying to get her riled up.

Glee danced in Joseph's eyes. "You know what this means, don't you? Blackwell is most likely a crook."

"How dare you impugn the man in his own house," Beatrice said through clenched teeth. "You are insufferable."

"So I've been told." Relaxing his arms but still leaning back, Joseph pulled out his pocketknife and began his loathsome practice of grooming his nails.

Trying to ignore him, Beatrice discarded one folder and chose another, her heart pounding with panic. Taking a few deep breaths, she forced herself to slow down and really study each piece of paper.

Joseph finished with his nails and moved on to cracking his knuckles. Beatrice realized that the former Lord Blackwell had been quite a collector. She found receipts for porcelain, glass, silver, tapestries, rugs. Ah, one painting, but not the *Madonna of the Garden.*

"We can give up, you know. Tell Horatio that Blackwell's collection is tainted, and we're on our way home."

"Absolutely not!" Joseph jumped at her bark. She even startled herself. "I am not satisfied that the paperwork doesn't exist. Since Blackwell is not here, we need to give him a chance to find it." The Biagi painting was the heart of the collection, the most valuable piece. The gallery—and Horatio—wanted it, and she wanted Blackwell to be able to sell.

Joseph scoffed at this. "You are entirely too trusting, my dear. It's obvious to me that Blackwell is suffering financially and is trying to hoodwink us." He waved at the papers, almost losing his balance but recovering. The chair legs thumped down. "How many of those items do you see around here, hmm? The Ming vases, for example. Where are they?"

"I haven't seen them," Beatrice admitted. The valuable four-hundred-year-old blue-and-white vases detailed on an invoice weren't on public view, at least.

"They're gone, I'll wager. So my advice is, we pack up here and take the train back to London tomorrow."

Objections flooded Beatrice's mind, jostling to be uttered: the unfairness of Joseph's verdict, the unseemly haste in abandoning their task, the loss of the collection to the gallery. Also to be considered was the loss of funding for the school. Beatrice had to admit she had grown to care about the school, despite her disagreement with Blackwell.

But what if Joseph is right? a little voice whispered. *What if Blackwell is a scoundrel, and you are a foolish woman taken in by his pretty tale of educating impoverished children?* The spectral cries of the infant and woman rang in her mind, and once again, she saw the menacing visage of the intruder in the old kitchen.

"I am sorry, Joseph," she finally said, forcing the words through a dry throat. "We must wait until the lord returns. He deserves a chance to explain."

Her colleague pushed back his chair with a muttered oath. "Have it your way. You'll see the truth of my words." He stalked out, leaving Beatrice alone with the pile of papers and ledgers.

She glanced up at the Madonna's serene smile, despair flooding her as hopes for a brilliant career crumbled. Then, more out of dogged fortitude than hope of success, she pulled a stack of correspondence closer. In the interest of being thorough, she decided she should retrace all of Joseph's work before conceding.

Beatrice searched through the papers for another hour, scanning each piece as quickly as she could to ascertain its contents before setting it aside. When the words began to run together, she realized she wasn't taking in anything anymore. She really should stop for the day and pick up again in the morning. Just one more stack, she decided, and then she would go out on the terrace for some much-needed air before dinner.

At a glance, the folder appeared to be personal letters to the present Lord Blackwell. She briskly shoved them aside, but then her hand hovered over the pages. What if there was something in there regarding the paintings? Something he wouldn't want them to read, perhaps, but something they should?

Whom did she owe more, her guardian and the gallery, or Lord Blackwell? One represented her life and livelihood; the other was merely a new acquaintance. However, propriety dictated restraint no matter how shallow the relationship. On the other hand, he had put the papers here for them to read, hadn't he?

Gritting her teeth against a sense of intruding upon a man's private affairs, she picked up the first letter. It was a notification from his tailor in York saying his new suit was ready. She snorted at her squeamishness. No secrets there.

The second letter was also personal but of far different character—and short enough that Beatrice read the entire thing before she could stop herself. The unforgettable words seared themselves into her mind.

Dear Isaac,

I pray you will find it in your heart to forgive me. I will spend the rest of my life atoning for my grievous error if you will give me another chance.

Your wife,
Lily.

13

Cabot Falls, Vermont,
Present Day

"Tell us what happened, Sofia," Julie urged. "What did Catherine say?"

"She said someone just called her—an unidentified male from a blocked number, of course—and told her he wanted one million dollars in cash. Instructions to follow."

"So they want money instead of the jewelry," Marla said.

"That's often easier for thieves," Thor said. "Selling rare jewelry can be difficult, since you need buyers who don't probe into the origin of the pieces. The selling process gives more opportunities for the police to catch the thieves."

"Yeah," Jim said. "Taking it down to the local pawnshop wouldn't work very well."

"The police always watch the pawnshops," Homer said. "At least, that's what Pat tells me." He smiled fondly at his wife.

"Catherine said the crooks warned her not to bring the police in on it," Sofia said. "Not only that, but using that method they would only recover a fraction of the collection's worth. I saw those pieces; they are exquisite."

David gave a long, low whistle. "So they believe Catherine can put her hands on a million cool ones right away. They must know something about her financial affairs then."

"Good point, David," Thor said. "A lot of very wealthy people don't have easy access to liquid assets. They might have to sell something to raise the ransom."

David's point reinforced Sofia's belief that the burglars had inside help. "Where should we start, Thor?"

Thor pulled out his phone. "Give me the names and anything you know about the people who live with or work for Catherine. I'll start with background checks."

"Even Katie Smith, the cook?" Pat's eyes were concerned behind her glasses. "She's a local girl, and I can vouch for her. She was sick and wasn't even there at the time of the theft."

"I'm afraid so, Pat." Thor's tone was kind. "I'm sure I'll be able to eliminate her right away. Or anyone else who is innocent."

Sofia, Julie, and Pat told Thor all they knew, including names, approximate ages, and relationships to Catherine. He promised to get back to them within a day.

"That's great, Thor." Sofia was relieved to have the help of a professional. "What should Catherine do? I told her I'd call her back."

"Why did she call you, anyway?" Jim asked. "Does she think you're a crime-solving expert?"

"I don't know," Sofia said slowly. "I didn't think about that. She certainly doesn't know about Thor yet."

"Don't mention me right now," Thor said. He nodded at his client. "I'm working for David. Catherine might regard that as a conflict of interest."

Julie's cheeks were red as she toyed with the remains of her bread, breaking it into crumbs. "Uh, Sofia, I might have said something about your experience solving mysteries."

"What? That I'm a caterer who figures out who stole the silverware?" Sofia laughed. "Anyway, thanks for doing that. Now we can get access to the scene, identify the perps, and clear David." She shot Pat a smile. "That's how you say it, right?"

Pat gave her a thumbs-up. "Right. Perps, short for *perpetrators*."

"Tell Catherine to write down everything she can remember about the call," Thor said. "The man's voice, any background noise, exactly what he said." His face was grim. "The best thing would be for her to go to the police. But she'll probably refuse since she was told not to involve them."

The next afternoon, Sofia was in her Suburban with Julie and Marla, heading to Lake Lucy to meet with Catherine, when her cell phone rang on the console. "That's Thor," Sofia said. "Julie, can you answer it and put it on speaker, please?"

Julie grabbed the phone. "Hello, Thor. We're on our way to Catherine's house now. I'm putting you on speaker."

"Good afternoon, ladies," Thor said. The others called greetings, Marla flushing as she did so. She and Thor had a dinner date that night, Sofia knew.

"I've been checking into our crew, and I've discovered something really interesting." He paused. "I can't find a Gil Masters of the right age or description anywhere."

The trio were silent for a moment. "Did you try Gilbert?" Sofia asked.

"Yes ma'am. Also Giles and Gilon. That last one is Hebrew. Those also use Gil as a diminutive, although Gil is often used alone."

"What does this mean?" Julie asked. "That he doesn't exist?"

Thor laughed. "That's what I'm thinking. Gil Masters is probably an alias."

Sofia considered this. Why on earth would a handyman be working under an alias? There had to be a reason, most likely a nefarious one.

Marla leaned forward between the seats. "So what do we do now?"

Thor considered for a moment. "The only thing we can do is find out who he really is. One method is getting his fingerprints. Maybe we'll get lucky and he'll be in the system."

Sofia stopped at an intersection and waited for the traffic to pass. She glanced at the others. "What do you think? Are you game?"

Julie's green eyes were wide with excitement. "I think so."

Marla nodded. "I am."

"Thor, we're going to try to get his fingerprints while we're at the house," Sofia said.

"Don't put yourselves at risk," Thor said. "It's not worth it."

"We'll be careful," Sofia said. "We'll try to get him to handle something for us."

"We'll do our best," Julie amended.

"That's right," Marla said. "I'll give you a report at dinner." Her cheeks flamed.

"See you then, Marla." Thor's voice held warmth. "Listen, I wouldn't say anything to Catherine about Gil right now. If he is a criminal, we don't want her confronting him or acting different and tipping him off."

"Good point," Julie said. "If I found out my employee might be a crook, I'd probably fire him right away."

"She's not in danger, is she?" Sofia asked.

"I don't believe so," Thor said. "And if we learn he's violent, then of course we'll tell Catherine immediately. Call me if you need me. And good luck."

Julie hooted after Thor hung up. "Hot date, huh?"

Marla smiled. "Well, he's better than that car salesman I went out with last week. He spent the entire time trying to get me to buy a new car."

Catherine answered the door immediately when Sofia rang the bell. "Please come in. I'm so glad you're here." The woman's usually immaculate hair was mussed, and she had lavender circles under her eyes. The situation was obviously taking a toll.

After introducing Marla, whom Catherine had not met, Sofia said, "I'm not sure what we can do, but we're happy to offer our support." She and the others took off their coats and boots, leaving them in the entranceway.

"I'm hoping you can help me figure out who did this terrible thing."

Richard came gliding down the staircase. "Mother, you know who did it. That security system man."

Sofia exchanged glances with her friends, who wore appalled and angry expressions. She raised her brows at them as a signal to play it cool. "The jury is still out on that one," she said. "I'm sure the police will figure it out."

Catherine's cheeks went white. "The police! You didn't tell them—"

Julie touched Catherine's arm. "Of course not. We've kept mum as you asked."

"Tell them what, Mother?" Richard's tone was sharp.

"Nothing important." Catherine's tone was evasive. "One of my vendors for the auction gave me a bad check when I asked for a refund. I'm trying to handle it without filing a police report."

Interesting. Catherine hasn't told her son about the ransom demand.

Richard didn't look convinced as he trailed along behind the women as they walked into the great room and sat down in front of the fireplace area.

"Would you like tea or coffee?" Catherine asked.

Sofia stood. "Why don't you relax, Catherine? I'll get it." She gave a little laugh, hoping to lighten the mood. "After all, I know my way around your kitchen."

"I'm sure you do, Sofia." Richard's voice held a note of insinuation. "You were able to become quite familiar with the house when you stayed over, weren't you?"

Sofia halted, spinning back to face the group, speechless. Was Richard implying that she and Julie had been involved in the theft?

"We stayed because the roads were bad," Julie said. Her normally animated voice was flat, almost grim. "That was the only reason. You know that."

Richard smirked in response, folding his arms across his chest and regarding each of them silently.

Julie shifted on the sofa. "We can leave, if you'd rather, Catherine."

Catherine put out a staying hand. "No. Don't go." She frowned at her son. "Richard, these fine women had nothing to do with the theft."

"They knew about the jewelry," he mumbled, his eyes shifty.

"So did any number of people," Marla said crisply. "It wasn't a secret, was it?"

"Who are you?" Richard asked, his gaze roaming over Marla in an almost insulting manner.

Matching him glare for stare, Marla sat up a little straighter and said, "I'm Marla Dixon, head librarian at Cabot Falls Library, and a good friend of Julie and Sofia's."

"They're my friends too," Catherine said, "so please keep your suspicions to yourself, Richard—"

"Whatever." The forty-something man shrugged like a teenager and lumbered to his feet. "I'll be upstairs if you need me, packing for Boston."

Sofia waited until Richard was halfway up the stairs before sitting down again. "I promise you, we didn't have anything to do with the break-in, Catherine."

"I know you didn't. I'm grateful for your support." Again the older woman hunched her shoulders and rubbed her hands together as if trying to get warm. "I can't raise that money for a few days. I told the man that."

"This is a little out of my depth, I must admit," Sofia said. "Maybe we should bring in the police."

Catherine's headshake was vehement. "No! I can't take the risk that they will disappear with my jewelry. They might even take the stones out of the settings and sell them loose. Then they will never be recovered."

"That's true," Julie said. "At that point, they'd probably try to recoup whatever they could."

"I'm glad you see it my way," Catherine said. "I'm working with my bank now to get the money together."

"What about your insurance company? Did you have coverage?" Marla asked.

If Catherine did, Sofia reflected, then she could take the payoff rather than try to get the jewelry back.

"I haven't called them again. They have the police report, and they're dragging their heels, of course." Catherine's wan cheeks flamed with color. "The adjuster had the nerve to suggest I arranged the whole thing myself! Besides," she added, "I want my jewelry back so I can sell it to some worthy collectors. Otherwise, it will disappear on the black market, or worse, be dismantled for the gems."

The only way to proceed, Sofia realized, was to identify the thieves or their accomplices before the ransom was due. The first step was getting Gil's fingerprints.

Sofia stood. "I'll put that kettle on. Who wants tea? Or coffee?"

Everyone voted for tea, and Sofia headed into the kitchen. After putting the kettle on the burner, she rummaged in the cupboard for the tea selection.

Julie padded in. "Have you seen Gil?"

Sofia shook her head just as the sound of a snowblower caught her ear. They went to the window overlooking the backyard. Gil, bundled in a hat and coat, was clearing a path down to the lake.

"I hope the police are done with those tracks," Julie said. "He's going right over them."

"I hope so too, although they don't seem to be that interested in them." Sofia nodded to a door at the opposite end of the room from the living room entrance. "I think his room is through that door. I'm pretty sure it leads to the garage, and he lives above that."

While Sofia rustled with spoons, cups, and a tray to cover any sounds, Julie left to check Gil's room, but within seconds she was back, shaking her head. "Locked."

"That figures. Although I would probably lock my door too, if I were him." Sofia reached into the refrigerator for milk and filled a small jug.

Catherine appeared in the doorway. "Marla and I have been having a lovely chat. I just wanted to check that you found everything all right."

"Yes, I did," Sofia said, placing a basket of tea bags on the tray along with the rest of the accoutrements. "After I fill the teapot with hot water, I'll be right in."

Julie found the sugar bowl and put that on the tray too, as if that had been her reason for being in the kitchen. "I know Marla takes sugar."

After Catherine went back to the living room, Sofia sagged in relief. She hoped Catherine hadn't overheard their conversation or noticed Julie's foray to the garage and Gil's apartment. Being an investigator was stressful. How did Thor manage to do it full time?

And they still needed to get Gil's fingerprints somehow.

Back in the living room, everyone chose a tea, and Sofia filled the cups with steaming water. They each doctored their cups to taste.

"I do love a hot cup of tea on a cold day," Julie said.

"Yes. And I love sitting by a roaring fire." Marla reached out her hands toward the blaze.

Catherine tugged an afghan around her shoulders, then took a sip of tea. "I haven't felt warm since the robbery. And after last night's call . . . well, I didn't sleep a wink."

"I don't blame you," Sofia said. "I was shocked to hear that someone is holding the collection for ransom." She reached into her tote for a pad and pen. "Can you tell me what happened exactly?"

Catherine gave a little laugh. "Oh my, this is official."

"I find writing down the details helps me see connections that I might not otherwise," Sofia said.

"All right then. Let me see." Catherine set down her cup and closed her eyes. "It was around seven o'clock when the phone rang—the house phone, not my cell. I glanced at the ID, and it said 'private number.' I often don't answer those, but I was expecting a call from a friend with an unlisted number. A friend in Boston." She paused.

"What was his voice like?" Sofia asked.

"Hmm. Normal, maybe a little gruff. Slight Vermont accent. He seemed to know it was me because he blurted out, 'We have the collection, and if you ever want to see it again, it will cost you a million, in cash, in unmarked bills.'" Catherine waited until Sofia had all that down.

Out of the corner of her eye, Sofia saw Marla was recording the conversation with her cell phone, and she raised her eyebrows once to let her know she noticed. "Go on, you're doing great."

The older woman sighed deeply. "It's not hard since the whole thing is etched into my brain." She sighed again. "Then he said he would be back in touch with instructions, and if I wanted to see any of it again, not to involve the police."

"That was it?" Julie asked.

"Oh, and they would be watching." Catherine shuddered and glanced toward the big picture window as if the thieves were lurking outside.

"They just wanted to scare you, I'm sure," Sofia said. She tapped her pen on the pad, thinking. "Did you notice any background noise at all?"

"Like what?"

"Music, voices, traffic, that kind of thing."

Catherine thought for a long moment. Then her eyes lit up. "Yes, I did, actually. I heard a few voices and clattering sounds in the background, and then someone called out, 'Score!'"

Julie snapped her fingers. "Hockey game. There was one on last night."

"So we know he might be a hockey fan," Sofia said. "That's a lot of people around here."

"The clattering noise, though," Marla said. "Bet it was beer bottles. Maybe he was at a sports bar."

The mention of beer bottles triggered a memory for Sofia. Gil drank beer, and as far as she knew, he was the only one in a house of wine drinkers. Maybe there were some empties they could snag.

Sofia picked up the teapot. "I'd like another cup. Anyone else?" Everyone assented.

"If you'd like something to nibble on, there are cookies," Catherine said.

"I'll help you," Julie said, jumping up.

In the kitchen, she whispered to Sofia, "What's up? I can tell the wheels are turning."

Sofia filled the kettle again and turned on the gas, using the noise to cover her words. "Beer bottles. Gil drinks beer." She cocked her head toward the garage. "Maybe there are some in their recycling."

They moved quietly to the garage door, and Sofia turned the knob slowly so it wouldn't rattle. Each of the garage's bays contained a vehicle, but along the closest wall was a row of garbage cans, and one was marked for recycling.

"I'll keep watch," Julie said.

Sofia went to the can and opened the removable lid, careful not to let it slip from her hand. Inside was a medley of cardboard, glass jars, tin cans, wine bottles, and, yes, beer bottles, the brand Gil drank. She reached inside to grab one by the lip so as not to smudge any prints.

A sharp intake of breath made her lift her head. Julie was contorting her face and nodding her head toward the outside garage entrance door, which had a window. Sofia glanced back that way.

Gil was headed right for them.

14

The Yorkshire Moors,
April 1850

Thoroughly exhausted by work and a lack of sleep, and bewildered by the letter from Blackwell's late wife, Beatrice had asked that dinner be brought to her room on a tray. She didn't know where Joseph was and frankly didn't care. Instead, her mind kept repeating the heartbroken words of Lily's letter. *Forgive me.* What had his wife done, and what bearing, if any, did it have on her death?

Someone knocked at her door.

"Come in." Beatrice put aside the novel she had fruitlessly attempted to read.

One of the manservants entered, carrying a tray, as Sarah hurried behind him like a clucking hen. Under her supervision, he set the meal on the table beside Beatrice's armchair, tugged on his forelock, and went out.

Sarah fussed over the tray. "I brought you a chicken breast in gravy, boiled potatoes, and the first peas from the kitchen garden."

"Thank you, Sarah." Beatrice glanced at the meal, her stomach clenching. Despite its appealing aroma and appearance, she wasn't sure she could eat a single bite. Before the woman could leave, Beatrice stopped her. "Sarah, tell me. Have you worked for Lord Blackwell long?"

Sarah halted, her back stiffening. She turned slowly. "No, miss. I've been here four years. I came right after . . ."

Her voice trailed off, and Beatrice guessed what she was going to say. "After Lady Blackwell died?"

Sarah's hands went to her apron, and she twisted them in the cloth. "That's right. Except for Mr. Wesley, we're all new."

Interesting. Had the former servants betrayed the lord in some way, or had he wanted to remove any reminders of the time of Lady Lily? Perhaps one of the servants had been involved in her downfall. Either way, it appeared there was no point in questioning Sarah about Lily's sins or her death.

"Wesley has served a long time, then?"

Sarah attempted a joke. "He's been here a century or more, it seems. Served Lord Blackwell's father and was a boot boy under his grandfather."

Perhaps she should talk to Wesley. If anyone might know about the provenance of the painting, he would, having been in residence when it was purchased.

Beatrice picked up her linen napkin, removed it from the ring, and spread it over her lap. "Thank you, Sarah. This looks wonderful."

Thus dismissed, the woman fluttered her way toward the door again. "Leave the tray there when you're finished, and we'll get it in the morning."

To her surprise, Beatrice managed to put away quite a bit of the tasty meal, and thus satiated, she climbed into bed with her book, a dull pastoral romance that lulled her mind into restfulness. For once, her sleep was undisturbed until a rap on the door announced morning tea.

It wasn't Sarah today; instead, the bashful Ettie brought her tea tray and, in the usual ritual, poured her the first steaming cup from the pot.

"Ettie, have you seen Mr. Norris this morning?"

The maid's hand jerked, causing tea to slop into the saucer.

"No mum, I haven't." Her eyes were wide and frightened. "Was I supposed to?"

"I'm sorry, Ettie. Of course not." Beatrice accepted the cup from the girl's shaking hand. "I was just curious, that's all. We have a lot of work to do."

"Yes mum." At the assurance that Beatrice didn't need anything else, Ettie hefted the dinner tray from the side table and hurried from the room, utensils and dishes rattling.

Whatever was wrong with the maid? Beatrice hoped the china would make it back to the kitchen in one piece. She shrugged and added the encounter to the list of strange events in the castle.

Downstairs, neither of the manservants had seen Joseph, and when she inquired about Wesley, she was told he was indisposed. Leaving orders for Joseph to join her in the gallery immediately once he came down, she went straight there and prepared to work. If the provenance for the Madonna painting existed, she would find it.

With half a mind, she flipped through ledgers, thinking about writing a letter of report to Horatio. Joseph's behavior had been extremely irregular from the beginning, and although a novice at on-site engagements, she knew for certain that Horatio wouldn't approve. Eloquent sentences expressing her outrage floated into her mind, denunciations of her colleague's attitude, behavior, and demeanor. Not to mention his insinuations of wrongdoing on Blackwell's part. The gentlemanly thing to do would be to accuse the man to his face, not behind his back.

Something struck her on the shoulder, and she jumped a foot. Heart thumping, she turned to see Levi standing in the doorway, both hands to his face, which wore an expression of horror.

"I'm sorry, Miss Kimble. I was trying to scare you, not hurt you."

"You did both, you rascal." Beatrice glanced down and noticed a small rubber ball lying on the carpet beside her chair. She scooped it up and bounced it in her palm. "I guess this is mine now."

His face fell, but he quickly recovered. "I suppose you should keep it. I don't deserve it now after misusing it so."

She laughed and tossed it to him. "I was joking. What are you doing this morning, Levi?"

"I was looking for Lord Blackwell, but they said he's away." He stepped over the threshold, apparently taking her words as invitation to enter.

"He is. I'm not sure when he's expected back." She thought the boy would accept her statement as dismissal, but he continued into the room.

"What are you doing?" He leaned on the back of the chair next to her, raising the front legs and letting them thump down on the carpet.

"I'm researching paperwork for that painting." She pointed.

To her relief, he abandoned the chair and wandered over to *Madonna of the Garden*, gazing up at it with reverence. "This one is my favorite."

"Mine too. It's a very rare painting to boot." She kept her eyes focused on the ledger, hoping the boy would take the hint—and his ball—and go. Although she liked the little chap, she had too much ground to cover to waste time in idle chatter.

"What makes it rare? Can you tell me?"

Annoyed, she looked up from the ledger, prepared to scold him, but the sight of his earnest face struck her heart. He had a charming sprinkle of freckles across his cheeks and nose, she noticed. Perhaps he was genuinely interested in art, so she owed it to him to nurture that. Was he so very different from herself as a small child? She thought not, remembering her awe the first time Horatio had taken her to the gallery.

The decision made, she put a piece of loose paper in the ledger to mark her place and closed it. Standing, she joined the boy under the painting. "Vittore Biagio is considered one of the finest painters of the Italian Renaissance." He wanted to know what the Renaissance was, and she explained before continuing. "See the sunshine illuminating the figures?" She indicated the areas she meant. "That is a skill that represents a great leap forward in technique." For contrast, she showed him one of the Byzantine paintings, which were flat in comparison to Biagio's technique.

"Another strength of his work is the way he painted human figures. See how rounded their limbs are, how realistic their skin appears."

He nodded, never taking his eyes from the painting. "It seems like they would be soft if you touched them."

"Yes, that's right." She paused, allowing the beauty of the tender scene to seep in. "Biagi didn't paint many canvases—or if he did, they were lost. That is why this one is considered rare. We're elated to add it to the gallery collection." If she could locate the provenance, that is.

"What's the gallery?" Levi asked. "Is it in London?" He sounded awed at the thought of the huge, storied city so far away.

Beatrice explained, enjoying telling the boy about the magnificent building housing some of the finest paintings in the world. How proud she was to be part of such a grand endeavor. "Perhaps you will be able to visit someday," she concluded, glancing at her watch. "But I really need to get back to work."

Levi frowned, scuffing the toe of his boot against the carpet. "Can I stay with you while you work? I promise I'll be quiet."

"But what will you do?" She could scarcely recruit him to help her search the papers, although she wagered his work ethic was better than Joseph's.

His eyes lit up. "I'll get a book from the library and read."

"All right, then. You can stay." Beatrice pulled out her chair and sat. "Maybe after lunch, you can walk down to the post office with me again. I need to send another letter."

Beaming with joy, he skipped out of the room. Beatrice's mind drifted back to the letter she needed to write to Horatio. She had promised regular correspondence, especially if she ran into problems. And so she had. *But how much should I tell him?* Joseph still had time to redeem himself, and she prayed he would. Otherwise, she would be forced to report his antics. How unpleasant that would be—certainly not the note on which to start a career.

"Today isn't as nice as the other day we came along here," Beatrice said to Levi as they strolled along the cliff path. The sky was overcast, and the sea was a flat gray expanse, the waves breaking sullenly against the rocky shore far below.

"You have to be careful of the sea frets on a day like this," Levi said. "They come up suddenly, and you can't see farther than your nose." He demonstrated by holding a hand up to his face.

"Sea frets? You mean fog?"

"Yes. Do you get fog in London?"

Beatrice spent the rest of the walk, to the first row of cottages in the village, telling Levi about the infamous pea-soup fogs London experienced. Fog from the Thames River was thickened with fumes from burning coal, creating a noxious yellowish mist that made some people ill.

Levi considered this. "Sea frets won't make you sick, but they might kill you."

Before she could ask him what he meant, a shrill voice cut in. "Levi. Levi! Get in here now!" A heavyset woman stood in a cottage doorway, a passel of small children swarming around her knees.

The boy's whole body sagged. "I have to go. My auntie needs me."

"I'm sorry to part ways." Beatrice patted his shoulder. "I enjoyed our time together. I hope I see you soon."

"I hope so too, Miss Kimble." With a wan smile, he trotted away and disappeared inside the cottage. The woman gave her a suspicious glare, then slammed the door behind her.

Viewing the hovel he lived in and the unpleasant relative the poor boy had to endure, Beatrice raised Blackwell in her estimation. It really was noble for him to take an interest, although the boy was uncommonly bright and agreeable. Would such a man really stoop to theft? It didn't add up.

Beatrice decided to avoid the docks area by taking a side street leading up the hill and back down to the post office. She had no desire to encounter the denizens of the seedy pub again, although she was half tempted to see if Joseph was there. He hadn't appeared at lunch, and no one seemed to know where he had gone.

Ann True, the postmistress, was the only person inside the shop. Her sister was nowhere in sight. When Ann spotted Beatrice, she bustled out from behind the counter toward the post office window. "Got another letter for London, do you?"

"That's right." Beatrice slid the slender missive across the counter. "All alone today? That must be hard." She wouldn't want to take care of the post office and store at the same time.

Ann grunted. "My sister is ill." She weighed the letter and announced the postage.

Beatrice paid her in coins. "Last time here, you asked if I was enjoying my stay at the castle."

"Well, are you?" Ann's grim face discouraged conversation, but Beatrice pressed ahead anyway.

"Yes and no." Beatrice sighed. "I've had some . . . strange experiences." She hoped by putting out bait that she could learn more about the castle and its residents.

Ann took the lure, crossing her arms and leaning on the counter, a spark of interest in her eyes. "What do you mean?"

"I've seen and heard things at night. Either the others there wander, or there are ghosts." Beatrice laughed merrily, as if to say it was absurd. "I had to get up to investigate, but I found no one. Most mysterious."

"Be careful about wandering around at night." Straightening, Ann wagged a finger at her. "That's how young women get into trouble."

"Is that what happened to Lord Blackwell's wife, Lily? Did she get in trouble?" Beatrice was taking a shot in the dark.

Ann gasped. "What a thing to say about the departed!" Her eyes narrowed. "Are you setting your cap for his lordship, is that it? Good luck with that, missy. The likes of you aren't fit to shine Lily's boots." The woman hurtled around the post office counter.

Beatrice hastily backed away toward the door, wanting nothing more than to distance herself from the angry postmistress. "I'm sorry, Miss True. I didn't mean anything." She turned and wrenched open the door, the bells jingling frantically. Tendrils of fog crept in, and Beatrice saw to her dismay that a thick mist had set in. But she had to get back to the castle, away from this nasty little village.

"Don't take the cliff path," the woman called out to her as she stepped outside. "You'll never make it in this fog. Go over the first stile on the left, and that path will see you home." Beatrice slammed the door shut with another clash of bells.

Drawing her cloak closer against the damp air, Beatrice crept up the cobblestone street, the thick fog preventing her from seeing more than a few feet ahead. Lights inside the houses glowed in the mist, and vague shapes passed by, revealing themselves as human or animal when they drew close. She kept her head down and her gaze averted, hoping to escape notice.

Her breath condensed in the chill, and droplets of moisture clung to her hair and garments. Still, despite the thickness of the fog, the air was much cleaner than in London, and it smelled of seawater and mud flats.

Beatrice reached the place where the cliff path joined the road and, despite unease about finding her way, continued on. What had Levi meant when he said the sea frets could kill? Because she might fall off a cliff, as Ann True warned, or because the fog cloaked nefarious deeds?

She continued uphill, scanning the tall, thick hedges for the stile Ann had mentioned. There it was, a low step built into a gate so people could easily go through. Beyond the barrier was wilderness, an empty stretch of undulating moorland. She stopped and considered. What if Ann had sent her this way on purpose, hoping she would fall into a kettle hole or a gully?

She shook herself, alarmed at these dire imaginings. After all, the woman had been good enough to warn her, despite being annoyed by her questions about Lily. She could go back to the village and seek assistance from someone else—she thought of the unsavory pub patrons with a shudder—or she could make her way across the moor to the castle. It wasn't that far, and surely if she kept the sound of the sea on her left, she would stay on course.

Lifting her skirts, she climbed the stile and jumped down to the soggy ground with a squelch of her boots. At first the heath appeared unbroken, featureless, desolate. Then she saw a path of sorts, a mere depression scarcely discernable in the dense mist that surrounded her like a shroud.

15

Cabot Falls, Vermont,
Present Day

Sofia's heart lurched into her throat at the sight of the handyman coming toward the door. It was apparent he was intent on coming into the garage, and if she didn't do something fast, he would catch her in the act.

The knob rattled as Gil pulled the door open. Momentarily blinded by the contrast in light between the dim garage and the bright day outside, he blinked for a moment. Then his gaze focused on Sofia, his brow creasing in puzzlement. Julie had ducked back inside the kitchen.

"Hi, Gil." Sofia decided to brazen out the situation. She closed the lid gently as if she had merely been putting something in the bin. "I made tea. Do you want a cup?"

He shook his head. "I'm all set. Thanks, though." He continued to march through the garage, pulling off his cap and gloves as he went. He thundered up the stairs, and a moment later, Sofia heard Gil's apartment door open and shut.

Sofia's heart was still thudding when she slipped back into the kitchen. Julie was bent over, arms to her middle, laughing silently. Tears slipped down her beet-red cheeks.

Marla entered the kitchen. "What's wrong with her?"

"Sofia almost got caught lifting beer bottles," Julie said, gasping for air.

Marla turned to Sofia. "Really? What happened?"

Sofia started to explain as she turned up the heat under the kettle so it would boil. Catherine must be wondering what on earth had happened to her tea.

"Should we go get the bottles now?" Julie asked.

"We need to find something to put them in," Sofia said. "I realized that once I was out there. Otherwise, what are we going to say? We're helping recycle by bringing a few bottles back to Cabot Falls?"

At this ridiculous remark, Julie began to laugh again, joined by Sofia and Marla. All three were weak with merriment, bending over and clutching their bellies. Then Julie elbowed Sofia. "Shh." She cocked her head toward the garage door. Footsteps were thumping down the apartment stairs. They managed to straighten their faces by the time Gil came in.

"Is the offer still good on that tea?" he asked pleasantly. He rubbed his hands together briskly. "I could use a warm-up."

"Of course, Gil," Sofia said. She turned off the heat under the kettle, which was beginning to shriek. "Do you want it in here, or will you be joining us?"

He glanced at Marla. "I think I'll join you."

"Oh no," Julie mouthed behind his back as he and Marla went back to the great room.

"Don't worry," Sofia said. "I have a better idea than the bottles." She handed Julie a plate of cookies. "Take these out. I'll be right there with the hot water."

With Gil in the living room, making eyes at Marla, who firmly resisted his flirting, the talk remained general. After a few minutes, Sofia asked, "What time is it?"

When Julie told her, she said, "Oh my. I've got to get home to help my daughter with the Winter Carnival."

As she had hoped, that broke up the party. Gil drained his

cup and set it back on the saucer. Stretching, he said, "I'd better get back to work myself."

"Let me clear for you, Catherine." Although the woman demurred, Sofia reached for Gil's cup and saucer, careful to touch only the saucer's edge, and set it on the tray holding the teapot.

Catching on, Julie said, "I'll help you." She stood and picked up the plate of cookies.

Carrying the loaded tray, Gil's cup carefully set to one side, Sofia bustled into the kitchen, intent on only one thing: getting that cup packaged safely and smuggling it out of the house.

The Pinot Painters were drinking mulled cider in the four-season room before heading to the Winter Carnival at the Cabot Falls Fairgrounds. The house resounded with the noise of their combined crews enjoying a snack in the kitchen. Mark Butler was expected at any moment, and although school was over for the day, Jim was still at a teacher meeting.

"I brought you a present," Marla said, pulling a folder out of her tote and passing it to Sofia.

"What is it?" Sofia asked, flipping it open. Julie scooted closer to her on the sofa so she could see.

"It's part of an exhibit write-up my contact at the National Gallery found. Just a photocopy, of course. They won't release the original."

Sofia glanced at the first page. "*An Exhibit of Early Italian Art*," she read aloud, "*by Horatio Kimble*. Beatrice's guardian."

Marla grinned. "Read the dedication."

"*With many thanks to the following scholars . . . and to*

Beatrice Kimble Stanhope, esteemed expert on Renaissance art."

"Stanhope!" Julie exclaimed. "There's a clue. Now we know Beatrice got married."

"That's right," Sofia said. "Maybe we can find out who she married and more about her life." She closed the folder. "I'll read this more thoroughly later. Thanks, Marla."

Julie raised her mug to Marla. "Good job."

The front doorbell pealed.

"That must be Thor." Sofia stood, setting aside her mug.

Julie smiled at Marla with raised brows. "I hope he likes the skier look."

"Shut up, you," Marla said, blushing. The powder-blue wool sweater and ski overalls she wore flattered her blond hair and blue eyes.

"I'll get it!" Matthew yelled from the other room. He had lately developed the habit of wanting to answer the phone and door all the time. Knowing he was running ahead of her, Sofia moved more sedately, her black ski pants swishing.

"Mom, it's Mr. Anderson." Matthew's eyes shone with hero worship. "Do you have any cool gadgets with you, Mr. Anderson?"

"Not today, son." Thor patted Matthew on the head as he stepped inside. He, too, wore ski gear—a navy blue parka and matching pants. He smiled at Sofia, a startling flash of white in his tanned face. "Actually I'm here to pick something up from your mom."

Matthew cast Sofia a skeptical look. "Really? Mom doesn't like gadgets. I even have to figure out her cell phone for her."

Sofia laughed. "That's right, you do, Matthew. Come on back, Thor. We're having hot cider in the four-season room."

Matthew ran to rejoin the other children as Sofia led Thor to the back of the house. She called after Matthew, saying that they would be leaving in about ten minutes and then collected the kids' cups and plates to take to the kitchen.

When she returned to her friends, she saw Thor had joined Marla on the sofa. He toasted Sofia with a cup of hot cider. "This is great. Hits the spot after a long day on the slopes." He took another sip. "So, I understand you managed to get some fingerprints."

"I hope so," Sofia said. She went to her tote and pulled out the plastic bag that held the teacup. "I was so nervous getting this out of the house. I wanted to run, but I had to make sure I didn't act strange. It would have been easier if I could have told Catherine what we were doing."

"Yeah," Julie said with a laugh, "instead of running off with her teacup. But you can return it when Thor is done with it."

"That's right. I'll see you get it back," Thor said as he took the bag from Sofia.

"I could never be a detective." Marla shook her head. "I don't have the nerve." She gazed at Thor admiringly. "How do you do it?"

Sofia winked at Julie, enjoying seeing her friend flirt with someone she liked as much as Thor.

Thor shrugged, a small smile playing about his firm lips. "After years in Special Forces, civilian work is a walk in the park." He peered into the plastic bag, then set it carefully at his feet.

"I suppose so." Marla's blue eyes were wide. "You'll have to tell me about some of your adventures sometime."

"What's wrong with right now?" Thor asked. He shifted a little closer to Marla on the sofa.

With Thor's attention on Marla, Julie feigned a swoon, and Marla giggled.

Sofia glanced at the wall clock. "We're on our way to the Winter Carnival, but you and Thor can stay here and talk if you want, Marla."

Thor took in their ski attire. "Winter Carnival? I thought you were all going night skiing."

"You should come with us." Marla put a hand on Thor's forearm. "It's really fun."

"Yes, and there will be a lot of snowmobiles there," Sofia added.

Light dawned in Thor's pale eyes. "I get it. Maybe we'll be able to make some progress on the case." He smiled at Marla. "While we're enjoying ourselves."

Out at the fairgrounds, the Winter Carnival's pageantry kicked off with a pedestrian parade of costumed schoolchildren and marching bands circling the track in front of the bandstand. Each child held an electric torch made to look like a flame, and in the blue winter dusk, the sight was stunning. Sofia spotted Matthew and Luke, both wearing snowman heads. She recognized them by Matthew's snow pants, which already sported a duct tape repair across the knee. She hoped he would outgrow them before he destroyed them with his rough treatment.

Mayor Samuel Goodson welcomed everyone, urging them to enjoy the food and visit the craft vendors set up in the big barn, to admire the ice sculptures local artists had been working on all week, and to watch the sporting events held on the grounds that night and the rest of the weekend. Then he concluded, "But the biggest event not to miss is the crowning of our Winter Carnival Queen later tonight. Nine o'clock, folks."

The crowd erupted in cheers and then dispersed. Jim appeared at Sofia's elbow and gave her a kiss. "Was that Matthew acting goofy in the snowman head?"

Sofia laughed. "Of course." Taking his arm, they walked toward the barn. Every year, Sofia liked to check out the crafts while Jim enjoyed eating a fire-roasted sausage sandwich with peppers and onions.

"Can you believe our little Vanessa is competing for queen?" Jim asked.

His voice cracked, and when Sofia glanced up at him, she saw his eyes were misty. In response, a lump rose in her throat. "I know what you mean. She's really growing up. They all are."

As if to belie their sentiments, Wynter came dashing through the crowd thronging the barn area. She was wearing Vanessa's jaunty and colorful fleece jester hat, complete with bells. Wynter couldn't get enough of things that made noise since her hearing had improved following cochlear implants.

Following on Wynter's heels was a laughing Vanessa, who reached out and snatched the hat. With a shout, Wynter attempted to grab it back. Then Vanessa spotted her parents.

"Hi, guys." Vanessa elbowed Wynter, who turned to look. "Mom, guess what? I forgot my shoes." She held up one foot, adorned by a clunky boot. "These don't exactly go with my gown." Vanessa needed heels to go with her dress and to wear to the dance afterward.

Inwardly Sofia sighed. A mother's job was never done. "I'll go home in a little while and get them."

"I'd go," Vanessa said, "but I have to work at the art club booth. We're doing face painting."

"Then you definitely don't need your hat." Wynter snatched it back and put it on. "I'm going to check out the ice sculptures with my friends." She ran off, followed by a more sedately moving Vanessa.

Inside the crowded barn, Sofia and Jim wandered from booth to booth, greeting friends and checking out the wares for sale, which ranged from winter sports gear to handcrafts to snowmobile accessories. At the far end, the food stalls beckoned, savory smells of roasted meat and french fries drifting on the air.

"This is getting almost as big as the summer fair." Sofia had to shout in Jim's ear to be heard over the chatter and noise of heating blowers. Her eyes met those of a man standing across the way at a snowmobile booth. Richard Brown, Catherine's son. While she watched, he set down the snowmobile helmet he was holding, turned on his heel, and forced his way through the tightly packed bodies.

She hadn't pegged Richard as a snowmobiler. And besides that, hadn't he said he was going back to Boston? Maybe their quick assumption about Gil being the only one involved was wrong.

Sofia chose a pair of beeswax candles and a set of handcrafted wooden spoons, keeping an eye out for anyone else from the Stanley house as she shopped. The only person she spotted was Katie Smith, browsing the outdoor survival gear booth. For one of her suspense novels, perhaps? It was noisy, hot, and crowded in the big barn, and Sofia was exhausted from the hubbub by the time Jim bought his sausage sandwich and they exited.

"This is so bad for me," Jim said. He took a big bite and chewed. "But so good."

"Don't worry, you'll burn it off in the cold air." Sofia glanced at her phone. "Do you want to find the Butlers and the boys? I'm going to run home for Vanessa's shoes."

Jim held out the sandwich. "Sure you don't want a bite?"

"No thanks. We had soup with split peas and ham before we came over."

He feigned dismay. "Your pea soup? And I missed it."

"Don't worry, I saved you plenty." Sofia gave him a kiss on the cheek. "I'll meet you backstage at the pageant." With a wave, she trudged off across the packed snow toward the parking lot.

Since almost everyone in town was at the carnival, the dark streets were practically deserted. Sofia made it home, found the shoes in a cloth bag resting in the front hall by the door, and was on her way back to the fairgrounds in record time.

The area where she had parked before was full, so the attendant waved her to the very back of the lot. She was finally able to squeeze the Suburban between a dual-wheeled pickup truck and another SUV. At times like these, she wished she had something smaller and more maneuverable.

After Sofia climbed out, careful not to nick the SUV's door with her own, she scanned the area to find the best path to the building hosting the pageant. Frosty air stung her nose, and she pulled her scarf up around her chin.

A sea of cars lay in all directions under dim sodium lights, but in a nearby open area where snowmobile trailers were stored, rows of snowmobiles were parked in anticipation of the races. Men and women stood in groups, talking and laughing, checking out the features on one another's vehicles.

Excitement tingled. Maybe the thieves—or their snowmobiles—were over there. She had every reason to cut through that way since it was the shortest and most open route. On the uneven ground, Sofia had to watch her step so as not to slip on a ridge made by a snowmobile or a slippery spot where snow had melted and refrozen. While she trudged along, she scanned the treads for the distinctive mark of studs.

Sofia stopped short. There they were, little holes in the otherwise caterpillar-type marks made by the tracks. She glanced around to see if anyone was nearby and was surprised to see Gil Masters talking to two other men, all three bundled in snowmobile suits. While she watched, Gil threw his head back and laughed, a gesture that made him so much more attractive than his usual grim scowl.

Sofia edged closer, wishing she could hear their conversation. An idea dawned. She tucked the shoe bag under her arm and pulled out her cell phone. Putting it on the night setting, she zoomed in, held her breath to keep the camera still, and took several shots of the three men.

Someone behind bumped into her, making her stumble forward. "Sorry," the man boomed, a big burly fellow. "I didn't see you there."

"That's all right," Sofia said. Seeing that Gil and his friends were looking her way, she scurried off as fast as possible without running.

Halfway across the lot, she realized she had dropped the shoes. *Oh no!* How was she going to find them in the dark? She stood irresolute, wondering if she should go back to the car and grab a flashlight. She realized it was entirely possible that one of the snowmobiles now throttling up might run over the shoes, packing them into the snow.

She had just turned back when a figure loomed up in front of her. *Gil.* He held the shoe bag in one hand. "Did you drop something?" he asked.

16

The Yorkshire Moors,
April 1850

Praying she was going in the right direction, Beatrice stepped onto the moorland path. Once she left the landmark of the gate, the thickening mist swirled around her, making it impossible to see more than a couple of feet ahead.

Her experience in London told her to keep her eyes where she was going—in this case, on the uneven, rocky ground. Her skirts brushed against the vegetation on each side of the track, so she lifted the fabric, not wanting it to get wet.

No sound penetrated the murk—not a bird's cry or a sheep's lament. What a contrast it was to London, where the noise was constant. The city had streetlamps and signposts too. Here, she had to take it on faith that she would eventually reach the castle.

On she trudged, doggedly climbing the uphill path. *Shouldn't I be there by now?* The afternoon light was fading, like a lamp behind a screen slowly dimming.

She stumbled as the track took a sudden downward turn, and the sound of rushing water suddenly filled her ears. Cautiously taking another step, she found herself on the brink of a rocky stream. A stone post stood on the opposite bank.

Maybe it was a signpost. Lifting her skirts even higher, she crept down the bank, not wanting to stumble on a loose stone or slip on the mud. A few rocks in the stream provided a precarious crossing to the other side.

Beatrice made it across, having only slipped once, and climbed the hill to the rough-hewn spire. It was a cross.

An eerie sense of foreboding swept over her. Had someone perished here—another unfortunate traveler through the mists, perhaps? Lettering was hacked into the stone below the crosspiece.

"Lily." With a rush of sorrow and horror, she realized Blackwell's wife had died here on the moor, in this lonely and forsaken place.

A large figure loomed out of the fog, making her shriek. "Sorry, miss, didn't mean to startle you."

As he drew closer, Beatrice saw it was one of the local men, dressed in homespun trousers and jacket, a kerchief tied around his neck.

Beatrice put a hand to her throat, trying to still her racing heart. "Perhaps you can help me. I'm on my way to Blackwell Castle."

A chuckle rumbled. "Oh well then. You've gotten off the track a bit." He pointed to her left. "Go that way, and you'll soon come to the gates. It's not far."

A rush of relief coursed through her limbs. It wouldn't be long until she would be safe behind the castle walls. "Thank you, sir. I'm much obliged for your help."

"Glad I could be of service." The man trudged off in the other direction, whistling.

As her steps quickened in anticipation of reaching her destination, she realized something. When the man lifted his arm, she had clearly spotted something odd, a flash of white on his wrist.

Bandages. The sort one might wear if bitten on the wrist. Had she just encountered the highwayman again? The idea made her shudder and her steps quicken.

After a short trek, the path intersected the road leading to the castle. As she traversed the remaining distance, eagerly searching for a glimpse of the castle gates, her mind whirled with dire thoughts.

If the cross was any indication, Lily had died at that spot. Had there been a carriage accident, perhaps? She pictured the vehicle tumbling into the water. *How dreadful!*

And that man—she was thankful that he hadn't accosted her, tried to rob her, or worse. She was never going to walk the moors alone again.

The gates were closed, but Beatrice slipped through the unguarded gatehouse and onto the main drive, picking up her pace when she reached better footing. She couldn't wait to sit by the fire and enjoy half a dozen cups of hot tea.

A short while later, warm and dry once more, Beatrice returned to the gallery and took a seat in front of the fireplace. She needed to continue searching for the painting's provenance. If she couldn't find it, she would have to face the possibility that Joseph was right. And how that idea stuck in her craw!

Around six o'clock, Joseph ambled in. He leaned on the fireplace mantel, resting one foot on the fender and hogging all the warmth from the fire. He had a habit of that, it seemed.

"Still plugging away, I see," he said. "When are you going to give it up as a lost cause?"

"When I have to, but not before." Beatrice eyed him sharply. "Where have you been?"

He shrugged, a small smile flitting across his features. "Around. Pursuing my own interests."

"Like drinking in the village pub?" The words escaped before she could stop them.

He dropped his casual pose and turned to look at her. "What a little snoop you are."

Inwardly, Beatrice quailed, but she attempted to sound authoritative. "Horatio did put *me* in charge of this project."

"That doesn't mean you have to monitor my every move," Joseph blustered. "I'm a free man, and there's no law against drinking in a pub."

"There is a problem if you're doing that instead of what you're being paid for," she said quietly. She noticed her fists were clenched and deliberately relaxed them. Oh, how she hated to confront people! Why didn't they just do what they were supposed to? The world would run much more smoothly.

He waved that away. "Neither of us will be paid. This job is a failure." He turned back to the fire abruptly and stared into the flames, rudely dismissing her.

Beatrice studied his stiff back, wondering if he was right. Perhaps they should cut their losses and go back to London. But it was too late to make arrangements tonight. She would have to wait until morning. If only Blackwell would return . . . She wanted to give him a chance to address Joseph's accusations.

Sick of the sight of him, Beatrice straightened the papers before sweeping from the room without another word to her obstinate colleague. High time for dinner and bed. What a long and miserable day it had been.

Ettie brought her a dinner tray, ducking her head shyly as she crossed the bedroom to set it on the side table.

Beatrice set aside the book she had been staring at, not absorbing a word. "Thank you, Ettie. That looks very good." The plate contained a cutlet and vegetables with a bread roll on the side.

"Thank you, mum. Will there be anything else?"

Beatrice picked up her fork, eyeing the maid. She was new, yes, but surely she had heard stories about the castle and its inhabitants. "Take a seat." She nodded at the chair on the other side of the table.

Ettie glanced toward the door as if rescue lay that way. "I'm not sure . . ."

"Just for a moment. If Sarah gives you any trouble, I'll tell her it was my idea."

"All right." Muttering and sighing, Ettie perched on the chair, smoothed her skirts, and folded her hands in her lap.

Beatrice cut a piece of cutlet. "Tell me about Lady Blackwell."

"What do you mean?" Ettie's eyes darted around the room. "I don't know much."

"Sure you do." Beatrice popped the meat into her mouth and chewed. "I came across the place she died today." Inwardly, she wasn't as cool and heartless as she appeared. The very thought of poor Lily dying on the moor made her blood run cold. But she was tired of rumor and innuendo. She needed the truth so she could assess Blackwell properly. Obviously his wife's death affected him greatly. She had seen the grief in his eyes the day they toured the west wing.

"She didn't die out on the moor," Ettie whispered. "She died in her bedroom, in the west wing. They brought her back here after the carriage accident."

"She was still alive when they brought her back? I thought she died in the accident." Shock jolted Beatrice as her preconceptions about Lily's cause of death shifted. "Her room was in that wing?"

"Yes. That's why it's been abandoned." Ettie cocked her head, considering. "And because of the fire too, of course. It's a right mess."

Beatrice dropped her silverware with a clatter. "You're not saying—" It was too horrible to contemplate.

"Yes mum. Her room was right above the kitchen, you see. She was bedfast and . . ."

Nausea lurched in Beatrice's belly as unwelcome images came to her mind. "How . . . how did the fire start?" Would Blackwell and Lily have reconciled if the fire hadn't stolen her life?

Ettie pursed her lips and nodded. "They said 'twas Crazy Harry." The girl made a gesture to convey that he wasn't in his right mind. "The kitchen wasn't used, you see, since the lord and lady went to the main wing for meals. But Harry got in there one night and started a fire in the fireplace. It got out of control and . . . well, it was too late once they reached Lily. The smoke drifted up through the flue and overcame her while she slept."

That was a mercy at least. Beatrice thought of the weeping lady in white she had followed into the west wing. She still didn't believe it was a ghost, but now that she knew Lily had died here, in the castle, her "appearance" made more sense.

Someone knocked on the door. "Come in," Beatrice called.

Sarah stuck her head around the jamb. Spotting Ettie, she frowned. "So that's where you've gotten to, girl. I need you downstairs."

"Sorry, mum." Ettie jumped up, flustered, her hands flying to her hair, her skirt, her apron as she tried to straighten her appearance.

"It's my fault, Sarah," Beatrice said as promised. "I asked Ettie to sit down for a little chat, to keep me company while I ate. Please don't be angry at her."

"As you say, miss." Sarah smoothed her hands across her own apron. "If you don't need Ettie anymore, I'd like to have her come with me, if that's all right."

"Of course. Thank you, Ettie. My compliments to the cook, as always."

The two servants left, the door clicking shut quietly behind them. Beatrice toyed with the remains of the meal, her appetite gone. Poor Lord Blackwell. *Forgive me*, the letter had said. To be betrayed by his wife—for that's what Beatrice believed had happened—and then to lose her so tragically.

But why post a cross out there if Lily died in the castle? There must be a reason. It all seemed to revolve around the west wing. And who on earth was this Crazy Harry? She thought of the hook-nosed man she had seen in the burned kitchen. Could that be Harry? Why was he still loitering at the scene of the crime?

A terrible thought pierced her like a sword. How likely was it for someone to experience a carriage accident and a fire within a short period of time? Not very. Had someone wanted Lady Lily dead?

When someone knocked on the door a short while later, Beatrice assumed it was one of the servants retrieving her tray. But when she opened the door, Joseph stood there.

Beatrice drew herself up in alarm. This was most irregular. "What are you doing here?"

He smirked. "I haven't come to assault your virtue, I assure you." His nasty smile deepened when her cheeks flushed in hot mortification. "I have come to tell you that I have made arrangements for you to return to London in the morning."

"What?" Beatrice stepped back involuntarily, and Joseph pressed his advantage by entering the room. "Why on earth did you do that?" Although she had come to the same conclusion earlier herself, his high-handedness bothered her.

Clasping his hands behind his back, he strode to the fireplace, where he stood with his legs braced in an assertive stance. He flipped his coattails up with his hands. "It is no longer safe for you here."

Her mind already full of dreadful ruminations about Lady Lily, Beatrice blurted, "Do you mean you think I am in danger of being murdered?" Perhaps he knew something she didn't.

Joseph appeared thunderstruck. "Murdered? What are you talking about?"

"I have discovered that Lily, Lord Blackwell's wife, didn't die in an accident."

His eyes narrowed in speculation. "So you heard about the fire, did you? I believe it *was* ruled an accident."

"Mere semantics. First her carriage crashes, and then a fire is started under her bedroom. Both could plausibly pass as unfortunate and accidental, except for their occurring so close together."

Joseph considered this for a moment, pacing back and forth in front of the fire, flapping his coattails as he went. He stopped in front of Beatrice, his face grave. "This theory only makes it more imperative for you to leave. The gallery can't afford to deal with someone like Blackwell—reputation-wise, I mean. Good grief, the man may have killed his wife."

Beatrice crossed her arms and regarded him steadily, refusing to be intimidated despite her own inner doubts. "You think that now. When you came in, you thought something else. What was it, pray tell?"

His brow furrowed. "I've learned some disturbing things about Blackwell's business practices." He gripped her elbow and shook it lightly. "You know that highwayman? He works for Blackwell."

Beatrice jerked her arm away, her thoughts reeling as she tried to make sense of this new information. "But . . . Blackwell chased him off."

"He had the wrong target. That's what I figure." He gave a jeering laugh. "Not even Blackwell would stoop so low as to rob his guests."

Her head throbbing, Beatrice sank into the armchair. This was all too confusing. Despite the logic of what she thought about Lily's death and Joseph's accusations, something inside rebelled against the idea of Blackwell as a criminal. Would a criminal care so deeply for an orphan boy and plan to educate him and others? Although she had seen the highwayman, she was sure of it. The bandage on his wrist was a dead giveaway. This time he hadn't bothered her. Because he knew who she was, perhaps?

She shook her head. Nothing added up. "Joseph, I think you

had better leave." She kept her gaze resolutely on the fire, not turning her head when he continued to stare at her.

Finally he seemed resolved. "Be packed and ready tomorrow."

She didn't bother to answer. Perhaps it would be best if she left. She needed Horatio's guidance desperately, even if seeking it meant her first assignment was a failure.

Lost in thought, Beatrice sat by the dying fire, the only light the glow of the coals. Outside, the waves shushed invisibly against the shore, a thick layer of clouds obscuring the stars.

The overcast sky was a perfect metaphor for this dark, oppressive place. Around her the silence deepened, along with the chill inherent in the stone walls. *How could anyone live here without going mad?* At that moment, she would have given anything for the noise and bustle of London's vibrant, if filthy, streets.

She allowed her mind to drift to her home, to the sound of barkers hawking wares in Covent Garden, to the constant *clip-clop* of hooves hitting the cobblestones, to the foghorns and whistles of ships passing on the Thames.

A wailing sound penetrated her reverie, and for a moment, she thought it was merely in her mind. No, there it was again—crying and sobbing and keening. It was similar to the wailing of the banshee in Irish legend, thought to portend death.

Anger bolted through her, and she jumped to her feet. How much more would she have to endure? Someone was intent upon tormenting her; that much was clear. Beatrice lit the oil lamp, her fingers shaking so much it took her three tries to light a match. After adjusting the lamp to a dull glow, she quietly opened her door and stepped out into the corridor.

As on the other night, closed doors extended down both sides of the hall, mirror images of one another. Holding her breath, she listened intently, the silence itself almost deafening.

After a few minutes, the sobbing started once more, the thin thread of sound drifting from the central hall where the west wing connected. Gathering her courage, she took her skirts in one hand and the lamp in the other and strode toward it, pausing now and then to listen. Tonight she would not rest until the so-called ghost was unmasked.

At the entrance to the west wing, a figure in a long white dress hovered. Beatrice gasped, her fingers suddenly sweaty on the lamp handle. Despite her expectation of seeing the weeping woman again, the sight of her was a shock.

When Beatrice finally forced herself to approach, the woman darted through the open door and into the abandoned section of the castle. Beatrice smiled grimly to herself. How convenient. Surely a real wraith would go right through a closed door.

As she had before, Beatrice followed the figure down the hallway, increasing her speed in hopes of catching up. Once again, the figure vanished into the dark up ahead, near the staircase to the floor below.

This time, Beatrice didn't turn back. She kept going, entering an area she hadn't explored yet, another long hallway appearing to hold only empty rooms.

The smell struck her first, a pungent odor of smoke and mildew. The fire in the kitchen must have damaged these rooms. Beatrice glanced into each dark doorway as she passed, guessing the woman must have gone into one.

Beatrice came to a room that was furnished. She stepped into the doorway, hesitant to step over the threshold, realizing something horrible.

Everything in the room was charred—the four-poster bed and its draperies, the thick velvet curtains, the fine Oriental rug. The last crunched under her feet, dissolving into cinders. The fire and smoke added their own terrible design in black to a once-rich display in red and gold.

She reeled in shock and almost dropped the lantern. This must have been Lily's room. After her head stopped whirling and she managed to drag enough air into her lungs, she forced herself to investigate more closely.

No one was hiding behind the curtains or in the wardrobe. Then she noticed an open door on the far side of the room, in the corner.

Satisfaction coursed through her veins, invigorating her and clearing the last of her confusion and dismay. The so-called ghost had gone in there, she wagered. And she would follow.

The doorway was narrow, with a flight of stone steps ascending from the opening in a tight spiral, the risers a little too tall for Beatrice's legs. She had to stop and catch her breath several times, and more than once, she trod on her skirt hem and almost tripped.

Where was the staircase leading her? She tried to picture the castle layout in her mind. Was she climbing one of the towers?

Finally she reached a small landing and a door. She reached out and grasped the handle. Should she investigate? Only the belief that the woman was out there led her to turn the handle and pull open the door.

Cold air hit her as she stepped through the doorway.

And then the door slammed shut behind her.

17

Cabot Falls, Vermont,
Present Day

Sofia stared up at the handyman in shock. Had he noticed her staring at him and his companions? He must have, or else how would he have seen her drop the bag?

Gil shook the cloth bag. "These are yours, right?"

"Yes, they are." Sofia reached for the shoes, a shiver running down her spine. Then she realized she was still holding her phone. Had he seen her snapping those photos? She prayed not as she hastily tucked the phone into her pocket. Through a dry throat, she croaked, "You just saved me trying to find these in the dark."

He handed her the bag. "Were you checking out the snow-mobiles? There are a lot of great models in the races this year."

"Not really. I was trying to find a shortcut." Sofia gestured toward the fairgrounds buildings. "I'm sorry, but I need to get these to my daughter. She's in the pageant, and it's starting soon."

Sofia turned to walk back toward the carnival. To her dismay, Gil fell into step beside her. "You mean Vanessa? Pretty girl." In the near-dark, his face appeared to be a grayish blur as he looked over at her. "I'll bet she wins."

"I hope so." Sofia's stomach churned. She didn't trust his suddenly friendly demeanor and wished he would go back to his usual taciturn self.

His next words made her knees wobble with relief. "Is Marla here tonight?"

So *that* was his interest in her. Then another thought struck her. *What if Gil saw Marla with Thor?* She had no idea how well-known the security expert was, but it wouldn't do them any good if the Stanley household knew Thor was on the case. Catherine didn't even know.

"I think Marla might be here somewhere," Sofia said with a brittle laugh. "She told me she was bringing her son." That was true, and maybe it would put him off.

As she hoped, his stride faltered. "Her son?"

"Yes, he's fifteen and a real handful." Sofia crossed her fingers against the lie. Tim was a sweetheart, gentle and intelligent, yet athletic, just like his late father.

"Well, tell her I said hi. See you later." With that, Gil veered off and went back the other way.

Sofia continued toward the pageant building, and as she passed the skating rink, she saw Marla and Thor circling arm in arm. That had been a close call. She detoured to the fence to call out to them.

Thor noticed Sofia waving and steered Marla over.

"Hi, Sofia. I'm having so much fun." Marla's blue eyes were bright, and her cheeks were pink from the fresh air and exercise. She threw Thor a happy glance. "I haven't been on skates in years, but Thor insisted I should try."

He smiled at her. "It's just like riding a bike. Your muscles never forget."

Sofia wasn't convinced of that, but she was glad Marla was enjoying herself. "I'm headed over to the pageant, but I wanted to give you an update." She filled Thor in on the studded tracks and the two men talking to Gil.

His easygoing manner dropped. "Forward those pictures

to me. I'll go see if I can catch up with Gil and company." He turned to Marla. "I'm sorry to interrupt our outing, but I really—"

"Say no more," Marla said. "I want to watch the pageant anyway. Maybe we'll catch up with you later."

He bent forward and gave her a quick kiss. "It's a plan. I'll text you." With a nod, he skated away.

"Want me to wait?" Sofia asked Marla.

"No, you'd better give Vanessa her shoes before she has a meltdown. I'll meet you over there."

Backstage, Vanessa was watching anxiously for the shoes, which were a perfect complement to her gown—pale green and white with with a spangled overlay on the flowing skirt. Her blond hair hung in loose curls, and Wynter had done her makeup to perfection.

"I was beginning to worry." Vanessa grabbed the shoes and gave her mother a kiss on the cheek. "Wish me luck, Mom."

Overcome by a swell of pride and love, Sofia grabbed her daughter tight for a moment. "We'll be rooting for you."

Wynter gave her sister a hug. "Break a leg."

Jim and the boys had saved seats for Sofia and Wynter; the Butlers were nearby, as were Marla and Tim. The six young women were announced, striding out onto the stage to cheers. After singing a medley of winter songs, each contestant was asked to make a speech with a winter theme. Vanessa spoke about her blue mittens, a special pair knitted by her great-grandmother, Elena Baresi. When she was eight years old, the blue mittens had gone everywhere with her—skating, skiing, sledding, and a trip to the hospital to welcome a new baby brother, Matthew—the string between them ensuring they wouldn't get lost. She brought down the house when she pulled the tiny mittens out of a hidden pocket and displayed them to the crowd.

No one in Sofia's circle was surprised when Vanessa won.

As applause and cheers filled the room, Sofia felt a rush of tears sting her eyes.

Jim's arms encircled her. "We'll always remember this moment."

Sofia pulled out her phone to take a picture of a beaming Vanessa on the stage, the crown on her head and a bouquet of roses in her arms, then noticed that she'd received a text from Catherine: *Please call ASAP! I've received ransom instructions.*

An hour later, Sofia was on her way to Catherine's lake house, accompanied by Jim, Marla, and Thor. The Butlers were taking care of the kids, watching the younger ones while Wynter, Tim, and Vanessa attended the Winter Carnival dance at the high school. They would make sure everyone made it home safely. Tim was going to stay at Sofia's for the night.

Thor's phone kept going off as more information arrived. "Oh my," he said, shaking his head. "Our friend Richard Brown is in way over his head."

Jim glanced at Thor in the rearview mirror from the driver's seat. "You mean financially?"

"That's right. He owes money to some really bad people." He whistled. "Make that a lot of money."

The pieces began to fall together in Sofia's mind. "Do you think he and Gil are in it together?" As they turned onto the narrow, dark lake road, her pulse sped up in anticipation of meeting with Catherine. How were they going to break this news to his mother? And what if Richard was at the house? That would be very awkward.

"Right now it's hard to say. I'm still waiting on some

information about Mr. Masters. Or whoever he is." Thor tucked the phone into his breast pocket.

"Maybe he's connected to those bad guys," Marla said. She clutched Thor's arm. "I'm so glad we have you to sort this all out."

Thor patted her hand. "I hope Catherine will be. We have to convince her it's the only way. She can't handle this alone."

"Thanks for coming so quickly, Sofia, Marla," Catherine said when she answered the door. Then her glance fell on Jim and Thor. "I'm sorry, but who are these gentlemen?"

"This is my husband, Jim," Sofia explained, "and his friend, Thor Anderson, a security expert. He's not in law enforcement," she added hastily.

Thor gave Catherine his warmest smile. "If you'll give me a chance to tell you what I know about your case, I think you'll find it worth your while."

Doubt creased Catherine's brow, but she stepped back, holding the door open. "Please come in, then."

As Sofia entered, she realized the house felt empty. The only lights burning were in the great room, where a fire roared. "Is Richard home?" she asked. "Or Melanie?" In fact, she hadn't seen the assistant since the morning of the robbery.

Catherine ushered them to the fireside seating. "Richard has gone to Boston, and Melanie is visiting her mother in Maine."

"Richard left you here to deal with the thieves alone?" Sofia's words burst out before she could rein them in. There was also the fact that she had seen him only a couple of hours before, at the Winter Carnival. Should she mention that?

"He doesn't know about the ransom demands." The older woman sank down into her usual seat on the sofa. By the looks of the empty cups and plates on the coffee table, she was spending most of her time huddled by the fire. "I didn't want to involve him in this mess," Catherine went on. Biting her lip, she stared into the crackling flames, blinking rapidly. By the sheen in her eyes, Sofia guessed she was holding back tears.

Marla caught on too. "Are you worried that he's involved, Catherine?" she asked gently.

Catherine nodded gently.

She wasn't the only one, Sofia realized. Katie Smith had said Richard fought with his mother about money.

Catherine fumbled for tissues to dry her eyes. After a few minutes, she muttered, "I'm sorry. You must think I'm a foolish old woman."

"Not at all, Mrs. Stanley," Thor said. "Having your jewelry stolen was a personal assault—a violation, if you will. The idea that a family member might be involved pours salt into the wound."

Catherine stared at Thor, apparently surprised by the big man's insights. "You are absolutely right. You see, all I have belongs to him, so why would he steal from me?"

"We don't know that he did." Thor's phone dinged, and he pulled it out to check the message. A smile of satisfaction quirked his thin lips. "Your handyman has a criminal record, so I say that makes him a prime candidate."

"The fingerprints worked, then," Sofia said. "I'm so glad."

"Fingerprints?" Jim asked, but then he shook his head. "I'm not sure I want to know." He softened the words with a smile and a squeeze of Sofia's hand.

Catherine's brows drew together. "Why did you collect my

employee's—or should I say my ex-employee's—fingerprints?"

"Ex-employee?" Sofia and Marla asked at the same time.

"He quit today." Catherine's mouth twisted in a frown. "It's like everyone is deserting me. Even Katie took the night off."

"No, not everyone." Sofia patted Catherine's shoulder. "We're here for you."

"That's right," Marla agreed sympathetically.

"Thank you both. You've been wonderful." Catherine smiled wanly.

"Back to Gil," Thor said. "We couldn't find him in the databases, so we suspected he was operating under an alias. We were right. His real name is Gus Mason, and he's a felon."

"I'm sorry for the subterfuge," Sofia said. "We didn't want to tell you our suspicions until we knew for sure who he was."

"That's right," Marla added. "Thor was worried Gil would notice a change in your demeanor toward him, and that might put you in danger."

"Good call," Catherine said to Thor. "I would have fired him right off if I suspected he had anything at all to do with the robbery." She shrugged. "But now we've lost track of him anyway."

"We'll find him," Thor promised.

"How did you come to hire Gil—or should I say Gus?" Jim asked Catherine. "It sounds like he targeted you as an employer on purpose."

Catherine shrugged. "I'm not really sure. A friend of a friend recommended him, and my other handyman had just left, so I snapped him up. Stupid of me, I know. Next time, background check." She jabbed her forefinger in emphasis, attempting a smile.

"Good idea, Mrs. Stanley," Thor said. "Now tell me about what happened tonight." He pulled out his phone to take notes. "Every detail you can remember."

"Well, I was sitting here trying to read a magazine, around

nine o'clock or so, when the telephone rang." She picked up the handset sitting on the coffee table and passed it to Thor. "Another blocked number. But I knew it was them, so I answered." She paused. "It sounded like the same man—kind of gruff, Vermont accent, not a voice I recognized. He asked me if I'd gotten the money together yet. I said I would have it by tomorrow."

"Any background sounds?" Thor asked, his thumbs working busily as he typed.

Catherine tapped her lip. "I really tried to listen hard. There weren't any background sounds like last time. You know, yelling or clanking. But I did hear one thing, near the end. It sounded like a recording of *Frosty the Snowman*."

"He must have been at the Winter Carnival," Sofia said. "They were broadcasting winter music." Gil and Richard had both been there, along with Gil's friends. She took a deep breath. "Catherine, I have to tell you something. I saw Richard at the carnival."

"What?" Two bright spots of color flamed in Catherine's cheeks. "He told me he was going to Boston." She covered her face with her hands. "Don't tell me he's involved with this mess."

The others exchanged glances over Catherine's bent head. "There's no evidence of that, Mrs. Stanley." Thor's voice was warm and reassuring. "So keep your chin up."

"I'll try," Catherine said. "It didn't sound like Richard anyway. I'd know his voice anywhere."

Sofia reached over and patted Catherine's hand. "A mother knows." Inwardly she prayed her platitude was correct. "What else did the caller say? Did he give you a drop location?"

The older woman's eyes widened in what looked like fear. "Yes. They want me to drop it at the gazebo across the lake tomorrow night."

"The one on the little island?" Marla asked. "You can only get there by boat in the summer."

Jim frowned. "They want you to walk all the way across the ice? Talk about an isolated spot."

"That is scary," Sofia said. "Thor, can we protect her out there?"

"No problem." Thor sounded confident. "The conditions that make it possible to get there also mean we can approach from any direction."

With a moan, Catherine covered her face with her hands. "I *can't* go there."

"We'll transport you if it's too far to walk," Thor said.

Catherine shook her head almost violently. "No, I don't mean it's not possible. I mean I just can't bring myself to do it. That spot is where my husband died."

How cruel. Did the thieves know that when they picked it? "I'll go," Sofia found herself saying. "We're the same height and weight. No one will be able to tell the difference at night."

"Are you sure you want to do this, Sofia?" Jim asked over the speakerphone. "We can always bail and leave it up to the police."

"I trust Thor," Sofia said. "He'll swoop in before anything can happen." She lifted her arms so one of Thor's female operatives could attach a wire to her undergarments. "Isn't that right?" she asked the woman.

"We haven't lost anyone yet."

"I wish I could be there." Jim sounded anguished.

"I wish you could too, honey, but it would jeopardize the operation." She turned at the woman's gentle prodding. "Someone is probably watching the house."

Thor and the rest of his team, including Jim, were at another house on the other side of the lake, closer to the gazebo. After dusk, Sofia had driven out to Catherine's, but the woman who left after half an hour or so was not Sofia. Catherine, bundled in Sofia's outerwear, drove the Suburban away. Along with the operative stationed at the house, radio transmitters and cameras had been set up for constant communication with Thor.

The agent made a final adjustment. "Go ahead, put your turtleneck on. That mic will broadcast through all the layers you'll be wearing." She studied Sofia critically, made a tweak to the box attached to her pants waist, and with a curt nod, left her alone to wait. And pace and pray.

An hour later, Sofia set off across the frozen lake, boots crunching on the crusty snow, her only companions a sliver of moon and the sprinkle of stars in the inky sky. Although appearing smooth and unbroken from a distance, the empty, windblown expanse was crisscrossed by snowmobile tracks, with occasional gray patches where ice was exposed. She had to step carefully to avoid slipping.

Sofia turned to look back at the Stanley house, where a solitary light burned. The rest of the shoreline was black, dense with trees. The island waited straight ahead, a small huddle of pines breaching the white. To her right was the outlet, where Catherine had warned that the ice was often thin.

Crunch, crunch, crunch. She trudged across the seemingly endless field of white to the island. A light burning in the trees to the left let her know that Thor and his people were watching.

"Can you hear me?" she whispered.

Thor's voice crackled in her ear. "Yes, we can. Hang in there, Sofia. Only a little farther."

"Tell Jim I love him." A smile curved her lips at the thought of the taciturn detective passing along that sentimental message.

She heard a muffled snort and chuckle, then a sheepish, "He loves you too."

The gazebo grew larger in her vision as she approached the island, the pines thrusting upward around it. She crossed the final stretch of ice, careful not to step into any patches of open water near the rocks, then walked up a small rise. She was on the island.

"I made it," she said softly, trusting Thor and the others would hear her.

During the summer, the gazebo was a delightful spot, smelling of evergreens and with a view of blue lake on all sides. Now the structure was a cold, forlorn shell, its frigid timbers creaking in the wind.

"No one is here yet," she told the others.

Sofia tromped up the snow-covered steps and stood shifting from foot to foot to stay warm, not wanting to sit on the bench, which was equally buried in the white powder. She was probably the only person to come out here all winter. After a few minutes, tired of the straps biting her shoulders, she slid off the backpack holding the ransom in inventoried bills. There had been much debate about that, but Catherine had insisted Sofia have the money on her. Otherwise, if things went wrong, she would be in danger.

Once in a while, she turned in a circle, scanning the sea of black and white for signs of someone approaching. Her ears were ringing, the night was so quiet, although the ice occasionally shifted on the lake with an ominous crack. Ice wasn't static, she knew from one of Jim's lectures to the kids. It changed continuously in response to temperature.

Then she heard a faint humming and looked up to see two pinpricks of light bouncing across the snow. The hum grew louder, resolving into the roar of snowmobiles. By their path, she could tell they were headed toward the island. No mere pleasure-seekers then.

"They're coming," she said into her microphone. "I hope you're ready."

"We see them." Thor's voice was reassuring. "We have your back." She heard muffled sounds, then, "Remember, hide your face as long as possible."

Sofia tugged her hat down, pushed her scarf up around her chin, and pulled the coat hood forward so it shadowed her face. Then she pulled out her flashlight and waited for the thieves to arrive.

18

Yorkshire Moors,
April 1850

The slamming of the tower door sounded like the clap of doom. Even as Beatrice tried the handle, she knew it wouldn't open. After setting the lamp on the flagstones so she could use both hands, she twisted the big brass knob again and again.

Nothing. She couldn't pull the heavy door open. She banged on the thick wood with her fists, shouting, "Let me out! Help!"

Silence. If someone had locked her in, they were long gone. She was trapped. But where exactly was she? In the lamp's glow, she saw a half wall about as high as her chest enclosing the area, with open windows on every side. Overhead was a square, pointed roof. She must be in one of the small towers that thrust up in the castle's facade like arrows.

A cold wind blew through, making her shiver. Why hadn't she put on a wool shawl before venturing from her room? All she had on over her nightgown was her lace shawl, and that provided almost no warmth.

Would anyone ever find her? She imagined herself dying out here and not being found for centuries. The legend of the missing art appraiser. She had read a story like that once, the tale of a bride locked in a trunk while playing a game. She must have pounded at the lid in vain while her bridegroom searched . . .

Panic trembled in her limbs as she darted to each wall, trying to see which way the tower faced. On two sides, she had views of roofs. Another overlooked the grounds, and the last, the road leading to the castle.

The lamp. She placed it on the windowsill next to the wall to make sure the wind wouldn't blow it over. Surely someone coming along the road would see it. Then she huddled on the hard, cold floor in the least windy corner, tucked her feet up under her, and wrapped the thin shawl around her shoulders. All she could do was wait.

Beatrice fell into a doze, the whining of the wind a background accompaniment to her uneasy dreams. Fire in a bedroom . . . the woman in white . . . the vast and empty moors . . . the cries of seagulls . . .

This last resolved into a boy's excited, high-pitched voice. *Levi.* "She *is* out here like I told you."

Another, deeper voice rumbled a reply, but she couldn't quite catch the words. Her eyes seemed glued shut, the effort to open them too much. Strong, warm arms lifted her, carrying her out of the tower and down the winding steps. Thinking it was just another dream, she snuggled closer, gripping the man's lapels between her fingers. She smelled horses and bay rum. *How nice.*

By the time they reached her room, she was awake. Levi opened her door, and Lord Blackwell carried her through, placing her on the bed and drawing the covers up to her chin before tending to the fire.

"You found me," she croaked, curling up into a ball. She was shaking from cold and shock, limbs twitching and teeth chattering.

"I heard Lord Blackwell was coming home tonight, so I sneaked out and came over to see him. I saw you go into the west wing," Levi said. "I tried to open the door, but I couldn't."

Feeling slightly warmer, she stretched out her legs. "Thank you, Levi." Beatrice looked over at Blackwell, who was standing by the fire, holding the poker. "And thank you, Lord Blackwell. I am pleased to see that you are back." Words about the missing provenance for *Madonna of the Garden* rose to her lips, but she thrust them down. How coincidental that he was here tonight. Would he have rescued her if Levi hadn't intervened?

"I just arrived home," Blackwell said. "I saw the lantern in the tower and was on my way to investigate when Levi told me where you were." He gave the logs a final thrust and placed the poker in the stand, then turned to face her, his face in shadow. "I'd like to discuss why you were up there in the middle of the night, but that can wait until tomorrow."

Beatrice rose to a sitting position, anger surging through her. *Oh, so that is how he is going to play it.* As if she had done something foolish, something wrong. Then she sank back. Perhaps she had. Visiting his late wife's bedroom would be construed as intrusive, no matter the reason.

He gestured to the boy. "Come, Levi. Let Miss Kimble get her rest. I'm sure she is tired after her exertions."

Beatrice bit her tongue. What an aggravating man he was.

Levi, who was hovering anxiously next to the bedside, darted forward and gave her a kiss on the cheek. "Good night, Miss Kimble. Sweet dreams." With a last glance back, he and Blackwell left her alone.

Beatrice touched the cheek where the boy had kissed her. What a sweet little thing he was. It was fortunate he had seen her go into the west wing. What else had he seen? If only she could ask him a few questions.

There was one person she could talk to—Wesley, the butler. Surely a sick man might welcome a nice visit from a lady.

She lay back down and snuggled deeper under the blankets. The best news was that since Blackwell was back, she could ask him about the paperwork for the painting. The deal might be salvaged yet.

"May I help you, miss?" The plump woman deboning a chicken carcass wiped her hands on her apron. The kitchen was long and dim, with tan walls and a series of small windows along the ceiling that let in the morning's dull daylight. Ettie and two other women were stirring vats, washing pans, and sweeping the floor. They all turned to stare at the intruder.

"Are you Cook?" Beatrice asked. The woman nodded. "I wished to tell you that I've really enjoyed the meals you've made me."

Cook ducked her head. "Nice of you to say, miss. Is there anything I can do for you?"

"I'd like to visit Mr. Wesley. I've heard he's poorly." Beatrice displayed the book of Wordsworth's poetry she'd found. "I thought I could read to him."

Cook darted a glance over Beatrice's shoulder, then turned to see Sarah hovering behind her. "Miss Kimble would like to visit Mr. Wesley," Cook said.

Sarah frowned. "He's quite ill." She crossed her arms across her chest.

Beatrice crossed her own arms. "Too ill for visitors?"

"Surely not, Sarah," Cook said. "Ettie was going to take him tea and toast. Why don't you go along, Miss Kimble?"

"Have it your way." Sarah made a disgusted sound and flounced off.

Her reaction confirmed Beatrice's belief that the old butler was the best source of information in the castle. Of course, he might be blindly loyal to Blackwell, justified or not, but anything she could learn would help her understand the situation better.

Ettie led the way up the back stairs to the servants' quarters, the dishes clattering on the tray. The butler's room was at the end of the hall, in the men's section. Ettie knocked with her elbow, then barged through the door, shoving it open with her hip.

Beatrice hovered in the doorway as the maid set the tray at the bedside. Wesley was lying in bed, the covers pulled up to his chin. "You have a visitor, sir. Miss Kimble. She wants to read to you."

The butler struggled to a seated position. "Miss Kimble. How good of you to come see an old man." His voice was hoarse, and the effort of speaking made him cough, a rasping bark. He hastily grabbed a handkerchief and put it over his mouth.

"Please rest, Mr. Wesley," Beatrice said. "I didn't come up here to make you worse."

Ettie giggled as she poured Wesley a cup of tea. She added a big dollop of honey to it. "We thought a visitor might be a tonic, sir."

Wesley waved Beatrice closer. She found a straight-backed chair and dragged it over near the bed. "That's right." To Ettie, she said, "I'll take it from here."

"Very good, mum." With a curtsy, the maid left.

After settling him with his cup of tea, Beatrice opened the book and began to read, the soothing and lyrical words like balm to her spirit. By the peaceful expression on the old man's face, she guessed they had the same effect on him.

"You're a treasure to take time to read to me," Wesley said after she paused for a break. "I know you're busy with the artwork." His broad smile illuminated his craggy face, giving Beatrice a glimpse of the handsome young man he must have been once.

Beatrice smiled back, quailing at the thought of disturbing the peace in the room with probing and no doubt unpleasant questions. "*Madonna of the Garden* is a fine piece," she said. *An innocuous way to start.*

"It certainly is," Wesley said. "I remember when the late Lord Blackwell, God rest his soul, brought it home. I was just a lad, in training to be a footman. We had a lot more servants in that day, not the skeleton crew we try to get by with now." He shook his head. "But times are hard. What can you do?"

"So you remember the first time you saw it?" Beatrice prompted.

Wesley's eyes lit up. "Of course. All of us assembled in the gallery for the unveiling. Lord Blackwell said he considered it the centerpiece of his collection. And so it is."

"Are you sad to see it go?" Beatrice felt a pang of regret at depriving the castle residents of something they had cherished for decades. *But many thousands more would enjoy it in the gallery*, she reminded herself.

"Of course. But I understand the need to sell it. I hope I'm not speaking out of turn when I say that my lord is between the devil and the deep blue sea. He can't maintain the estate as it was in his grandfather's day. It's time for something new."

"Like the school."

The butler closed his eyes. "Like the school." He was silent for so long that Beatrice thought he had drifted off to sleep. Then he roused. "I'll be happy to see the Madonna safe in the National Gallery." He paused again. "Don't let *them* have her."

"Who do you mean?" Beatrice asked.

But the old man merely snored in response.

It would be too cruel to wake him. Beatrice quietly put the chair back, picked up the book of poetry, and slipped from the room.

She retraced her steps down the servants' hallway, thinking furiously. She needed that provenance now.

As she reached the head of the stairs, her heart lifted when she saw a familiar figure bounding up two steps at a time. Lord Blackwell. Then she remembered his promise to probe into her reasons for exploring the west wing, and her spirits fell. It seemed they were always rubbing each other the wrong way. That moment of rapport in the west wing, discussing the school, had been all too fleeting.

When he reached the top of the stairs and saw her there, he stopped short, grabbing the railing for balance. "Miss Kimble. What are you doing up here?"

She brandished the book, glad to direct the conversation to the butler. "Visiting poor Mr. Wesley. I thought a little poetry might make him feel better."

"How is he? I was just on my way to see him."

"He's fast asleep." Before he could say anything else, she moved toward the stairs. "I'll be on my way, then."

"Wait, Miss Kimble. I have a bone to pick with you."

Here it came. She decided to bring up her own problem with him. "And I have one to pick with you. I regret to tell you that I'm having trouble locating the chain of ownership for the *Madonna of the Garden*. Without it, the deal will be off, of course."

A series of emotions—disbelief, dismay, anger—ran over his face. He clenched one fist. "I told you, it should all be there. I've seen it myself. I don't know what kind of game you are playing, Miss Kimble, but it isn't pleasant."

"I assure you it's not a game. I'm serious and most discomfited to encounter such a situation at great expense to the trustees."

That remark hit the spot. Rubbing his chin, he averted his eyes, staring instead at nothing off to one side. "I really don't know what to say. The paperwork must be misplaced."

"Well, you'll have to help me look for it." Her tone was tart, but she didn't care. "I've looked through everything. And so has Joseph."

Joseph. Something clicked in her mind. Who had sown seeds of doubt about their patron's integrity? Claimed the paperwork was missing? Tried to get her to leave? A sense of certainty rose out of her belly, a deep intuitive knowledge. She smelled a rat, and his name was Joseph.

"Never mind," Beatrice said, pushing past him. "Let me check one more thing first." She felt Blackwell's eyes on her back as she hurried down the staircase. With any luck, she would be able to explain shortly.

Beatrice checked the gallery as a formality—no Joseph, of course. The boxes and ledgers were the way she had left them the day before. According to one of the manservants in the hallway outside, Joseph had gone out, and so had Blackwell. For once, Joseph's absence didn't anger her.

Claiming to need a rest, she went upstairs, but instead of turning left to her room, she turned right, into the north wing. Joseph's room was along here somewhere.

Tense with the fear of discovery, she stole softly along the hallway, opening each door. Most of the rooms were empty and dark, curtains pulled shut to prevent sunlight from fading the precious rugs and fabrics.

She recognized the room belonging to Lord Blackwell immediately as soon as she smelled bay rum. She knew she shouldn't loiter, but for some reason, her hand lingered on the door handle. The heavy walnut furniture was carved and polished as befitted nobility, the headboard of the bed an immense arch, and thick carpets covered the floor.

In contrast to the rich furnishings, the room had an empty, almost Spartan feel. There were no personal possessions in view beyond a Bible on the bedside table and a silver hairbrush on the bureau.

A creaking sound in the hall made her jump. How terrible it would be to be caught snooping in His Lordship's private chamber. She closed the door hastily and moved on.

Joseph's room was the last one on the right, sharing the same view of sea and sky that hers enjoyed. His belongings were strewn about—a jacket flung over a chair, shoes tumbled next to the bed, the wardrobe door hanging open.

She hesitated a moment, knowing that her intrusion

represented a serious breach of etiquette. What if she was wrong? A brief review of the previous few days told her otherwise. Holding her breath, she stepped inside and closed the door softly behind her. She needed to be quick. In and out, like a thief. Or rather, like a detective.

She began with the obvious, his valise. She found an assortment of clean underwear and socks, which she handled between pinched fingers, her stomach churning in distaste. She lifted the pillows on the bed and reached under the mattress. Nothing. She even bent and lifted the spread to peer underneath.

The bureau drawers were empty. That left the wardrobe, where a pair of trousers, a jacket, and a couple of shirts hung. On the shelf above were a few men's hats, apparently left there by someone else since they were of a style popular decades ago.

On a whim, she pulled them down, one after the other. And then she struck gold. A sheaf of papers was rolled and tucked inside a beaver top hat, pushed up against the crown. With shaking fingers, she gently tugged them out, careful not to tear the brittle pages.

Certificato di vendita. She didn't know much Italian, just enough to confirm that this was the bill of sale for *Madonna of the Garden.* Her theory was right; Joseph had removed the papers in an attempt to discredit Blackwell and prevent the sale.

But why?

Before she could come up with anything, the door to the bedroom burst open. Beatrice shrieked, almost dropping the papers as she whirled around to see who was there.

Joseph stood in the doorway, a gloating expression on his face.

19

The Yorkshire Moors,
April 1850

"I guess you're more clever than I gave you credit for." Joseph leaned against the doorjamb, arms crossed, one knee cocked in a parody of relaxed good humor.

Her heart pounding, Beatrice shook the bill of sale at him. "Why do you have this? You removed it from Blackwell's paperwork, didn't you?"

"That, my dear, is a very complicated question. One I don't have time to answer right now." He gestured, and two men appeared behind him. With a start of surprise, Beatrice recognized burly Ned from the pub and the moors and the hook-nosed man from the west wing.

Ned waved a pistol at her, an evil grin on his face. "Hello again, missy. Sticking your nose where you shouldn't, I see."

Beatrice darted a glance at Joseph before returning her gaze to the deadly weapon. "What are you doing, Joseph? Surely you can't be serious."

At his nod, the men moved into the room, each grabbing her by an arm.

"Serious as Napoleon at Waterloo." Joseph snatched the papers from her hand. "I'll take these." He nodded at the other man. "Tie her hands, Harry."

"Are you Crazy Harry?" Beatrice asked. He certainly looked the part.

"That's right, mum." Harry gave her a horrible grin as he pulled down a curtain tie and used it to fasten her hands behind her back while Ned kept the pistol trained on her. In the meantime, Joseph moved about the room, throwing his clothes and other belongings into the valise. He crumpled the provenance and threw it into the grate, which held banked coals. He watched with satisfaction as the paper flared into flame. "I won't be needing that anymore."

Beatrice gasped and tried to run toward the fireplace—not that she would be able to do much with her hands tied—but Ned held her back. She squirmed and kicked, managing to connect with Ned's knee.

Ned swore and tightened his iron grip. "You're a wildcat, you are."

"Calm down, Beatrice, or we'll tie your feet too and carry you," Joseph warned.

Beatrice subsided. *But only temporarily*, she told herself. "You're going to steal the painting, aren't you? I think Blackwell will have something to say about that."

Ned's foul breath blew into her ear. "Don't worry about His Lordship. He'll be well taken care of."

Harry rubbed his hands together. "I hope we get to burn something again." He cackled. "I liked watching the pretty flames."

Horror trickled down Beatrice's spine. Was her theory correct, that the fire in the west wing wasn't an accident, and that Lady Lily had been murdered? She swayed on her feet when she realized something even more dreadful.

Was she next? And what about Lord Blackwell?

"Shut up, Harry." Joseph tossed him the valise. "Let's go."

Ned steered Beatrice toward the doorway. She dug in her heels, but his strength was too much for her. She screamed as they entered the hallway, praying someone would hear her.

"Keep it up and we'll gag you." Joseph led the way to the staircase, striding along the carpet like he owned the place. Walking with her hands bound behind her back wasn't easy, and to get down the stairs safely, she had to balance by leaning against the bannister. She didn't trust Ned to save her if she fell. He would probably just as soon see her break her neck.

At the foot of the stairs, Beatrice spotted Sarah coming across the great hall, and despite Joseph's warning, she cried out. "Sarah, Sarah! Help me! These men are kidnapping me!"

What happened next shocked her to her core: Joseph slapped her across the face, and Sarah smiled.

"How are things coming in the gallery?" Joseph asked Sarah. He rubbed his palm as if the blow had hurt his hand.

Sarah sketched a curtsy. "Very well, my lord. Everything is being carefully placed in the wooden crates as you asked."

Everything! It seemed they were stealing the entire collection, not just the Madonna.

"I'll be along soon," Joseph said. "Don't let them hammer the tops on until I inspect their work."

"Very well, sir." Sarah bowed again and scurried off toward the gallery.

Despite the stinging in Beatrice's cheek, she blurted, "Why on earth did she call *you* 'my lord'?"

"Because I'm entitled to it." Joseph laughed. "Get it? En-titled?"

"You're as deranged as Harry," she said. That was the only explanation that made sense. For some reason, Joseph felt he had the right to Blackwell's possessions and station. And these poor deluded fools were along for the ride.

Joseph put his face close to hers, his eyes glittering. "Actually not. Check Burke's Peerage. You'll find my lineage in there." He referred to the directory detailing the family trees of landed gentry throughout the United Kingdom.

Beatrice scowled back at him. "Surely it's beneath you then, as a nobleman, to steal Blackwell's art?"

"Not if it's legitimately mine." Joseph gestured to Ned and Harry. "Come on, time's a-wasting."

Ned gave Beatrice a shove between the shoulder blades, and she stumbled forward, Joseph's revelations spinning in her mind. She was forced to reevaluate everything she knew about him. In London, he'd made no pretension of nobility, claiming instead to be the son of a poor clergyman who had attended university thanks to a small inheritance. And there was no disputing the fact that even if he was telling the truth about his family, he was breaking the law now. Noble birth couldn't justify that.

Beatrice wasn't surprised when Joseph led them into the west wing. Everything wrong at the castle seemed to center there.

"Light a torch," Joseph told Harry. "It's dark as a tomb in here."

"You're the one who tried to make me believe the castle was haunted," she said to Joseph as Harry shambled toward a wall torch. "The crying baby, the woman in white, shutting me in the tower . . . that was all you, wasn't it?"

The torch flared, casting shadows across Joseph's face. "It wasn't literally me, but yes, I planned it. Too bad you didn't take the hint." He shook his head in mock sorrow. "I tried to get you well out of it, I honestly did." To Harry, he said, "You'll have to bring that along. We're going down below now, and the others will need the light."

Beatrice's faint hope that someone, anyone, would come along and help her dwindled into despair. "Where are you taking me?" she cried.

"You'll see," was Joseph's terse answer.

With Harry holding the flame aloft, the group made their way deeper into the west wing along deserted hallways. Harry lit wall torches as they went, his gleeful laughter as each ignited making Beatrice's skin crawl. Where was Blackwell? Surely he would stop this madness.

Unless he was hurt—or dead. Waves of sorrow and fear swept over Beatrice. What were they going to do to her? The best situation was they would leave her behind when the gang left the castle with the paintings.

But that wasn't likely. As long as she could identify the thieves, she was a threat, especially to Joseph, since he was the ringleader. He couldn't risk her returning to London and raising the alarm.

They went down stone steps to the basement, which had vaulted stone ceilings and a flagstone floor. As they trudged deeper underground, the passageway narrowed, and cool, damp, briny air touched Beatrice's face. They were headed toward the sea.

"Are we in a tunnel?" she asked.

Joseph sighed. "Inquisitive as ever, I see. Yes, we are."

"This leads right to the cliffs," Ned added helpfully. "It's very useful when we get shipments in. We can carry them right up to the castle or into the village."

"Without Lord Blackwell's knowledge, I assume," Beatrice said.

"Of course he doesn't know." Ned sounded offended by the idea. "He's a straight arrow, quite rigid in his views."

"Shut up, you fool!" Joseph barked.

"What difference does it make, my lord, since . . ."

Beatrice's worst fears were confirmed. They had no intention of allowing her to live. A sudden weakness rushed through her limbs, making her knees sag. She would have collapsed onto the ground, but Ned steadied her.

From somewhere deep within, a new fortitude rose inside Beatrice. She wasn't going to give up without a fight. Instinctively she hid her resolve. Let Joseph think she was merely a weak-willed female led to slaughter like a lamb.

They went through a thick wooden door barred with iron

and emerged in a vast cavern, which hadn't been hewn by human hands. The walls and the ground were made of rough, uneven rock that gradually became sand, and the ceiling overhead was so lofty, it was lost in shadow.

The air was cold and dank, and the smell of the sea was stronger. At the far end, daylight spilled through a tall opening, and they emerged onto a wide, pebbled shore. A large wooden dinghy with two sets of oars was pulled up on the sand, out of reach of the encroaching tide. The cliffs towered overhead, and seagulls wheeled and cried as they dove toward the heaving gray water in search of food.

Joseph led them down the shore to another, smaller opening in the cliff. The water was already lapping the entrance, and the tallest members of the group had to duck to get inside.

Lord Blackwell lay propped against a boulder, mouth gagged, hands and feet tied. To Beatrice's relief, he seemed otherwise unharmed.

"I've brought you some company, Isaac." Joseph's laughter was both sly and triumphant.

Blackwell's face grew red with rage, but the gag muffled his angry words. Ned dragged Beatrice beside Blackwell and forced her to sit. He pulled a piece of rope out of his pocket. "Just in case you decide you want to walk out of here." He bent and tied her ankles together so tightly that the rope dug into her skin.

"Do you have to make it so tight?" Beatrice wiggled her feet, hoping the circulation wouldn't be cut off. Blackwell moaned and writhed, trying to convey his displeasure. "Does he really need a gag? There's no one for miles."

"True." Joseph reached down and pulled it off. "I might as well allow you two some conversation while you wait for the tide to come in." He laughed again. "Perhaps you can confess your sins to each other."

The tide! Beatrice glanced around the small cavern. The walls were glistening wet well above their heads, and barnacles grew on the walls and floor. Her heart clenched.

Blackwell's voice was a croak. "Worry about your own sins. They are legion."

Joseph propped his hands on his hips and cocked his head. "Whatever do you mean? The Biagio rightfully belongs to me."

"Your grandfather, Lord Swinton, lost it to mine fair and square on a horse race wager." Blackwell glowered, a grimace that bared his teeth. "I thought I recognized you the first night we met. You're the spitting image of him."

"So I've been told. But I'm not as naive as Grandfather, unfortunately for you." Joseph turned to the other men. "It's time to go."

"You're right," Ned said. He shaded his eyes with the flat of his hand. "I see the ship coming now."

Beatrice followed his gaze. The masts of a ship appeared near the horizon.

Joseph rubbed his hands together in glee. "We'll be in France by nightfall." He leered down at Beatrice and Blackwell. "As for you . . . the sea will be your shroud."

"You won't get away with this," Blackwell called out as Joseph walked away.

The other man whirled around and gave them a salute. "That's what they always say. But in this case, you're wrong. Goodbye, Blackwell, Beatrice." Then he seemed to reconsider and came back into the cave.

Was he going to let them go? Apparently not, for he stopped and loomed over Blackwell, hands on his hips. "I have one last thing to tell you. It doesn't seem fair to let you go to your grave without knowing." He paused, seeming to enjoy the suspense he was creating.

"Spit it out, Norris," Blackwell growled. "You know you want to."

"Your wife. Lily. She wanted out at the end. But we couldn't allow that, could we?"

At his words, the truth exploded in Beatrice's mind. Blackwell's wife had been involved with Joseph and his gang of smugglers. And they had killed her.

"You scoundrel!" Blackwell attempted to lunge at Joseph but was unable to do more than roll around. "You'll hang!"

Joseph shook his head, sneering. "I don't think so. I will be safely in France tonight."

"What did you have over her?" Beatrice asked. "I sincerely doubt she assisted you out of love." She invested her words with as much venom as she could muster.

They hit the target, for Joseph's face flushed dusky red. "We were third cousins, and I knew much about her youthful indiscretions. When she had an opportunity to marry you, Blackwell, I let her know that her first loyalty was to me." He was fairly spitting with rage. "And then she changed her mind . . . was going to tell you—"

"Enough," Blackwell said, sounding weary. "You've won. You stole my wife, my paintings, and soon, my life. And that of another innocent woman. What more do you want?"

"You're right. I have won." With that, Joseph strode out of the cave.

Fear beat in her chest. Beatrice took deep, gasping breaths, knowing that to give in to these dire emotions wouldn't help. They were still alive, weren't they? With a massive effort, she managed to calm herself. If she succumbed now, she would cry until the seawater mingled with her tears.

"Dear Beatrice," Blackwell said gently, "I'm so sorry you ended up in the middle of my mess."

Her heart lifted at his endearment. "I am responsible too. I brought him here." She sighed. "I should have known something was wrong when we couldn't find the provenance."

He scoffed. "Why? For all you knew, I was the rogue, not your colleague."

Beatrice shifted uncomfortably. That was exactly what Joseph had implied, and she had fallen for it. "I'm so sorry for doubting you. Deep inside, I knew a man who loved children wouldn't fund a school through stolen art." Tears began to slip out. "I'm so sad that you won't be able to start your school. What will become of Levi?"

His gaze was tender. "What an extraordinary woman you are, to care about an orphan."

Beatrice gave a short laugh. "Oh, I'm not so special. I am an orphan myself and fortunate to have loving guardians." Would dear Horatio ever know what had become of her?

To her surprise, Blackwell gave a long, low, piercing whistle. "That would have been harder with a gag."

"What are you doing?"

Before he could answer her question, Levi appeared out of the gloom. At Blackwell's nod, he pulled out a knife and began to saw at his bonds.

"Careful now . . . that's it." Blackwell's hands came apart, and he used the knife to release Beatrice, then cut the rope around his ankles.

A rising joy filled Beatrice as she rubbed her wrists and ankles. They wouldn't drown in the cave. But some other people were about to find themselves in deep water.

"Here she comes," Beatrice whispered. "Get ready."

The trio had followed hidden trails back to the main cavern. They spied on the gang of thieves as they carried the most valuable contents of the castle out to the beach and loaded them onto the dinghy for transport to the larger ship. In addition to Joseph, Ned, and Harry, the servants Sam and Sarah and the barmaid, Dot, from the village were involved. Blackwell guessed the other servants had been locked up in the house, a theory that Levi investigated and confirmed before he was sent to fetch the Royal Coast Guard.

Now, accompanied by the other manservant, who swore he was loyal, they waited for Dot to come along the passageway to the large cave, carrying a small crate of silver. Blackwell leaped out and subdued the woman, clapping a hand over her mouth. "Quiet. The jig is up, Dot. Cooperate, and I'll tell the judge to go easy."

She darted ferocious glares at them but went meekly enough back to one of the dungeons where, with the help of a servant, Blackwell gagged her and locked her in. Then Beatrice put on the woman's apron and bonnet to prepare for the next stage of their plan.

"Do you think Levi has reached the watch station yet?" she asked as they reentered the large cave.

"I'm figuring he should have by now. It will take them a little while to get here." Blackwell carried a pile of timber to the entrance of the cave. Night was falling fast, and they were able to remain out of view of the others.

"Where do you suppose Dot has gotten to?" Ned asked, his loud voice carrying across the beach.

"Don't worry about it," Joseph said. "If she doesn't make it, worse luck for her." He glanced around. "I'm more concerned about Harry."

"I'll go look for him," Sam said. "He's probably sleeping in the castle somewhere as usual."

Beatrice and Blackwell exchanged glances. "At least we'll be able to reduce the numbers," Blackwell whispered.

When Sam strolled into the cave, Blackwell hit him on the head, and he and the loyal manservant, Evan, dragged him in and tied him up. Then Blackwell went back to the opening, where he lit a piece of kindling and tossed the flame into the pile of dry wood. It caught immediately and began to crackle.

Beatrice ran outside, making sure she stayed far enough from the illuminating flames that they couldn't identify her. Putting on a Yorkshire accent, she cried out, "It's Harry! He's setting the rest of the art on fire!" She ducked back inside before they could recognize her.

As they'd hoped, Joseph and Ned sprinted across the beach to investigate. After kicking out the fire, they ran into the cave. Ned was holding the gun.

The servant launched himself at Ned, who fell to the ground with a grunt. A shot rang out, and the bullet hit the ceiling of the cave, sending rock chips flying. The distraction allowed Joseph to shrug off Blackwell's grip.

"You don't give up, do you?" Joseph snarled as he slid a long, narrow blade out of his pocket. Darting forward, he slashed at Blackwell.

Blackwell managed to move his arm in time, but his sleeve was sliced open. He grabbed a large stick and swung it at Joseph's arm, trying to make him drop the knife.

Joseph lunged and Blackwell stepped back. Despite Beatrice's yelled warning, Blackwell tripped over a boulder and fell. Joseph was on top of him immediately, the blade held to Blackwell's throat.

Without conscious thought, Beatrice picked up a heavy rock with both hands. She dashed out of the shadows and, with a wince, thumped Joseph on the head. Apparently her aim was good, because Joseph groaned and the knife slipped from his fingers. The servant had finally managed to tie up the belligerent Ned, and he came to help Blackwell secure Joseph.

"We did it, Miss Kimble." Blackwell grabbed her about the waist and spun her around. "We aren't floating in the briny deep with the fishes."

Beatrice laughed with joy. "Thanks to Levi—and you, Lord Blackwell."

"My given name is Isaac. I do wish you would call me that."

"Isaac. That is a good name. I will, but only if you call me Beatrice." He set her down, and she paused to take a couple of deep breaths. "And so, *Isaac*, we saved the art from going to unscrupulous collectors in Europe."

He smiled. "Now I can sell it to you and start my school, *Beatrice*." A grave expression passed across his face. "The mystery of Lily's death is also solved." He crossed himself. "May she rest in peace."

Beatrice crossed herself too, deeply sad at the poor young woman's untimely demise. "I am so sorry for your loss," she muttered.

"Beatrice," he said, hesitation in his tone, "this is probably highly premature and perhaps inappropriate to discuss, but would you consider joining me at the school? If I take in girls, I could use a wise and level head like yours."

Excitement mingled with an odd disappointment in her breast. "You mean as a teacher? Why, that is quite an honor."

To her surprise, he dropped to one knee, gazing up at her while he clasped both of her hands in his. "No, my dear, I mean as my wife."

Before she could answer, Levi appeared next to them. "Say yes, Miss Kimble. Then you can adopt me." His freckled face was woebegone yet hopeful.

Beatrice burst into laughter and gathered them both into a hug. "How can I say no? I would be blessed to marry you, Isaac, and to have Levi as our son."

20

Cabot Falls, Vermont,
Present Day

$\mathcal{S}$ofia's heart raced as she watched the twin headlights of the snowmobiles approach. Each foot of ground they covered brought the confrontation closer.

"You're going to make it in time, right?" she whispered into her microphone. "They're almost here."

"Don't worry. We're in position," Thor said.

Sofia braced herself as the snowmobiles halted about fifteen feet away, close enough for a quick getaway. Two figures clambered off the machines. Even silhouetted in the snowmobiles' lights, Sofia could tell they were dressed in thick snowmobile suits and wearing full-face helmets.

She hefted the backpack, making sure to keep her head ducked down. One of the figures gestured to the other, and they both stepped up onto the bank and began trudging toward her, waddling awkwardly in their heavy gear.

They stopped short of the gazebo. "Do you have the money?" It was a man's voice, muffled by the helmet.

In answer, she hefted the backpack again. The thieves exchanged glances, and Sofia knew that not answering verbally had aroused their suspicion.

"Catherine. Is that you?" A woman's voice. Sofia couldn't quite place it.

They charged toward her. She whispered, "Game's afoot," then switched on her flashlight, hoping the beam would blind them and help block her face. Recognition jolted at seeing Gil's scowl through the face shield. She moved the light slightly to catch his companion's face.

Katie Smith? Catherine's cook and the daughter of Pat Cooper's friend was the second thief. The shock made Sofia's hand lurch, and she almost dropped the flashlight.

Katie took advantage of the moment to shine her own flashlight into Sofia's face. Wincing at the sudden glare, Sofia threw up her hand, but not soon enough. Gil spewed muffled curses; then, with a few long strides and a leap up the gazebo steps, he reached Sofia's side.

"What are you doing here?" Gil grabbed Sofia's shoulders and shook her. "Where is Catherine?"

Sofia screamed and tried to free herself from his iron grip. The real question was, where were Thor and the team? "She's at home. The money is in the backpack."

"Grab it," Gil said to Katie. He shook Sofia again before releasing her. "You've made a big mistake getting involved in this."

"So has Katie." Rubbing her sore shoulder, Sofia turned to look at the woman, who had knelt in the snow and was now unzipping the backpack. "This is going to break Pat Cooper's heart."

Katie snarled up at her. "So what? That old bag has a bad habit of sticking her nose into my business. Now that Mom's dead, it's even worse."

Being physically accosted by Gil was bad enough, but outrage flooded Sofia at Katie's cruel words. "You're lucky she cares. Especially since, for once, she's been a bad judge of character."

Katie sneered. "She's a fool. And so is Catherine Stanley. She dotes on that rotten son of hers. How does such a creep luck out having a wealthy mother?" Her words were laced with venom. "I wasted the best years of my life taking care of mine, and she was a hateful old battle-ax. Didn't leave me a dime, to boot."

"So you're going to even the score?" Sofia guessed.

"That's right. You've got to take what you want in this world. No one gives it to people like you and me."

"Enough banter," Gil said. "Is the money there?"

Katie pawed through the backpack as Gil directed his light inside. Bundles of green bills fastened with paper bands filled the compartment.

"There's the money," Sofia said. "Where's the jewelry? Deal's a deal."

A crafty expression slid across Gil's face. "Yeah, and Catherine blew the deal by sending you."

Katie stood and placed her hands on her hips, getting right in Sofia's face. "Yeah. So we're keeping the jewelry. Ha-ha. Sucker!"

Sofia had the feeling they wouldn't have returned the jewelry even if Catherine had shown up. *No honor among thieves, right?*

"Let's get going," Gil said. "No point in hanging around."

"Don't you want to count the money?" Sofia asked, mainly to stall them. *When are Thor and the team going to show up?* The last thing she wanted was for these two to disappear with the money *and* Catherine's collection.

"Nah," Katie said, sliding the pack strap onto one shoulder. "We're not going to bother. I know Catherine wouldn't cheat us. 'Cause if she did . . .'"

Fear for Catherine trickled down Sofia's spine. There was no doubt in her mind that Katie Smith was seriously unhinged.

"Give me that," Gil said, putting his hand out for the pack. "Get on your machine."

Katie glared at Gil, but she obeyed, sliding the pack off and handing it to him, then clumped down the gazebo steps. Gil turned to Sofia. "You wait here until we're gone, you hear me?

And if you're smart, you'll forget you ever saw us." He gave her a dreadful leer. "That is, if you want your family to stay safe."

Rage surged through Sofia at this threat to her loved ones, but she somehow held it in check. No sense in escalating the violence. She glanced over at the shoreline for the twentieth time.

At last! A faint roaring sound of motors across the lake indicated that Thor and his team were on their way.

One leg over the snowmobile body, Katie noticed too. "Someone's coming, Gil!" she screamed. She cranked the engine and then started off. "Woo-hoo!" she whooped. "South America, here we come!"

Gil ran to his machine, shrugging on the pack as he went. He jumped on and started the engine, following Katie as she headed the opposite direction from Thor's base.

More engines around the lake roared to life, and as Gil and Katie started across, a circle of headlights glazed simultaneously, like a convergence of searchlights from every direction.

"You're all right now," a voice said behind Sofia. "Thor got them."

Heart thudding with shock, she whirled around to see a man emerge from the woods. He was carrying a rifle. One of Thor's operatives.

She put a hand to her chest, breathing deep. "I didn't know you were there." Thor had said they were watching, but she hadn't realized what he meant.

"Jed Bates at your service." He gave her a little salute. "You were never alone, ma'am."

Sofia sank down onto the snow-covered bench, not caring if the wet cold seeped through her ski pants. Now that the confrontation was over, she felt drained, all the adrenaline that had buoyed her suddenly fleeing.

"Care for a hot drink?"

Sofia glanced up to see Jed offering her a thermos cup of

steaming coffee. "Thanks." She took it and sipped, appreciating the warmth of the brew as it traveled through her body. Then he handed her a few squares of chocolate, perfect for fighting possible shock. Plus it was the creamy imported kind.

Out on the lake, the circle of pursuers tightened, forcing Gil and Katie to the far right side. Sofia sat upright. They were all headed for the outlet, where the ice was treacherously thin. "Oh no. They're going to fall through the ice!"

Jed's voice was a comforting rumble. "Don't worry. Thor has everything planned to a tee."

The lead snow machine—presumably driven by Gil—pulled up as the ice cracked. Katie's vehicle, right on his tail, almost hit Gil's, barely managing to avert course. Katie's screams filled the air as the pool of black, icy water opened and the snowmobiles began to submerge. Thor's people roared over to help, stopping short of the spreading hole in the ice. Figures swarmed around the downed criminals, shouting, carrying ropes, and working together to rescue the trapped thieves.

"Shall we go over and join the party?" Jed asked.

"You mean walk?" Sofia stood, brushing snow off the back of her pants.

"Nope." Jed walked into the woods, and a few moments later, a snow machine roared around to the front of the island where Sofia waited. He handed her a helmet. "Hop on."

Sofia obeyed, feeling like an actress in a James Bond film as she climbed on behind the security officer. Jed throttled up, and they sped across the lake, the helmet's visor and Jed's bulk protecting her from the icy wind.

When they were halfway to the scene, flashing blue lights appeared on the lake road leading to Catherine's house. Thor must have called the police and emergency medical services. Within seconds, officers and EMTs were trudging down to the lake.

As their snowmobile drew closer to the scene, Sofia saw Gil and Katie, soaking wet and shivering, wrapped in blankets and carried away on gurneys accompanied by officers. Another pair of officers appeared to be examining the backpack with Thor and Jim.

Jed slowed his machine and Sofia saw people turning to watch their arrival. Jim recognized her, and he broke away from the others to run over to her. When he pulled her into his arms and gave her a huge kiss, Sofia felt exactly like a film heroine. She had ended up with the good guy—not like poor Katie, who was following the bad guy all the way to jail.

Sofia pulled tiny beef Wellingtons out of the top oven and set them on the granite counter next to Julie, who put them on a platter and passed the savory bites to Marla for a drizzle of horseradish sauce.

"Those look awesome, Mom." Vanessa pointed to the angels on horseback, oysters wrapped with bacon and then grilled. Like the Pinot Painters, Vanessa wore a tailored white shirt and black pants, although bib aprons covered the older women's outfits. "Shall I serve these?"

"Please. I'm sure they're all starving." Sofia flew over to the table where she had started compiling cucumber sandwiches.

Vanessa hoisted the platter and gracefully sauntered out into Catherine's great room, where chattering, laughing guests mingled, waiting for the jewelry auction to start.

Sofia glanced out the window toward the lake, noticing a few lazy snowflakes. She hoped the event would be over and everyone safely on their way before dusk.

Marla followed Sofia's gaze. "Don't worry, we're just getting flurries." She shook the bottle of sauce and continued dressing the appetizers. "I hope."

They all laughed.

Placing the last piece of beef on the charger, Julie stood back and regarded her work with satisfaction. "I'm so glad everything worked out for Catherine. By the sounds of that crowd, the auction should go really well."

"Thanks for helping out in here, Julie," Sofia said. "As the PR director, you really should be out there schmoozing." One of the girls Sofia had hired was sick, leaving her shorthanded.

"No problem," Julie laughed. "My boss is taking care of that." She glanced around at their preparations. "What next?"

"I think we're done for now," Sofia said. "Vanessa and her friends will serve all of this, so we can take a break for a few minutes." Sofia ran through a mental inventory. After the auction, coffee and an assortment of desserts would be served. An extra refrigerator in the garage held miniature pastries and cookies, and the coffee was ready to go with the touch of a button.

Catherine entered the kitchen, followed by Richard. "Everything is fabulous, Sofia," she said. "And the girls are doing a great job." As if conjured by her words, Vanessa and two of her high school classmates came into the kitchen and picked up the remaining appetizers.

Richard grabbed a Wellington as they went by and crammed the whole thing into his mouth. "Yum."

"I'm glad to hear that, Catherine," Sofia said. "I have a great team."

Catherine smiled warmly at Sofia and the others. "Yes, you do. I'll be passing along your name to friends of mine. Some of them host catered parties here at the lake."

Sofia's heart lifted. She was always happy to hear about more work. "That's wonderful. I'll leave some business cards with you." She had just had a new batch printed, another step confirming that she had a viable business underway.

"You can cater for me," Richard said. He found a plate of rejected appetizers that were lopsided or falling apart and began eating them one after the other.

"You're going to hold events?" Sofia tried to keep the surprise out of her voice.

Richard smiled smugly. "I'm opening an art gallery in Cabot Falls. I'll feature local artists, of course, but I'll also be bringing up some art from Boston. Best of both worlds. I'll have openings almost every month, so I'll need a caterer." He shrugged. "Appetizers, maybe small plates."

"I'd be happy to do it," Sofia said. She exchanged excited glances with her friends, who gave her several thumbs-up.

"I'm going to be Richard's silent partner," Catherine said. She patted his shoulder fondly. "One good thing to come out of this mess was a better relationship between us."

"Yeah, after she got over suspecting me of burglary, it was all good." He laughed and ducked when she swiped at him.

A bell jingled in the other room, signaling the start of the auction.

"That's my cue," Catherine said. "I have to go make my introductory remarks."

Sofia and her friends shucked their aprons and went into the great room to watch. Once again, the intricate beauty of the Victorian jewelry impressed Sofia, especially the millefiori, the multicolored glass designs. The jewelry was on display in locked cases around the room guarded by Thor's operatives, and as each came up for bid, high-resolution photographs of the pieces were displayed on a big-screen television behind the auctioneer.

In addition to bidding by the people present, two staff members from the auction house took calls from out-of-town bidders. The fast pace created tension and excitement that was almost palpable. Sofia felt her chest tighten in anticipation as each piece escalated in price and was sold with three raps of the gavel. By the barely suppressed glee on Catherine's face, Sofia guessed the prices were higher than the owner had hoped. The representative from the children's wing at the hospital looked equally happy.

Marla's phone beeped in her hand. She glanced down, then scrolled with her thumb, reading. She smiled.

"Is Thor calling in a bid?" Julie joked. Marla had expressed disappointment that Thor hadn't come to the event, but Sofia knew they had a dinner date planned for later in the week.

"No, silly. It's for Sofia." Grinning, Marla handed the phone over. "I just got an email about Beatrice Kimble Stanhope. Look what my contact found."

Sofia took the phone. Marla had opened a document that was attached to the email. It was a digital copy of a newspaper clipping, enlarged for easy reading. Dated 1891, the headline read, *Blackwell School Celebrates Anniversary.*

Along with the article was a photograph of two men with a woman standing between them. The woman was tiny, with gray hair pulled back into a bun. She had large eyes behind spectacles, a bow-shaped mouth, and a solemn but sweet expression. She wore a black lace shawl over her high-necked dress. On her right was a handsome, clean-shaven man with salt-and-pepper hair; on her left, a younger, slighter man with a goatee and a mischievous air even the formal portrait couldn't quell.

The caption read, *Lord and Lady Blackwell with their adopted son, Levi, on the fortieth anniversary of the boarding and day school for deserving pupils.*

When she closed the file, intending to hand the phone back to

Marla, she noticed a second article. This was really unbelievable.

Quaking with excitement, Sofia gestured for her friends to follow her. Busy with the auction, no one noticed them leave the room except Vanessa, who raised an inquiring brow. When they were gathered in the kitchen, Sofia showed the first article to them.

"That's wonderful. Your ancestor helped found a school," Julie said, looking at the phone.

"Both boys and girls. That was uncommon in those days," Marla commented.

"Yes, it's noteworthy," Sofia said. "But that's not all." She took the phone back and moved to the next news story.

Art Historian Foils Criminal Plot, announced the headline. The text continued, *Miss Beatrice Kimble, refined London lass and student of art under National Gallery trustee Horatio Kimble, stopped the wholesale looting of Lord Blackwell's Renaissance collection by local thieves.* The article went on to detail the caper. The wedding announcement of Beatrice to Isaac Stanhope, Lord Blackwell, was in another article from the social section.

Vanessa stuck her head into the kitchen. "Mom, they're ready for coffee and dessert." She noticed their rapt expressions as they studied Marla's phone. "What's up?"

"Your ancestor stopped a ring of art thieves," Julie said.

Vanessa's eyes were wide. "Is that a story about the quilt?"

"Yes," Sofia said. "The lace shawl. It became the eighth square in Nonna's quilt. Beatrice Alice Kimble Stanhope was an art lover *and* solved a crime."

"That sounds like someone I know." Vanessa gave her mother a hug. "Thanks for clearing Ethan's dad. I guess Nonna knew what she was doing when she gave you the quilt." With that, she picked up a platter and went back into the main room.

Marla picked up one of Sofia's business cards. "Hmm. Maybe you should add 'detective agency' to this," she joked.

Sofia laughed. "Only if you agree to become my associates."

"Let's call ourselves the Pinot Private Investigators," Julie said, picking up the thread.

"On that note, let's celebrate." Sofia poured each of them a glass of sparkling wine. She raised hers in a toast. "Good friends, good food, and—good gravy, it's snowing again!"

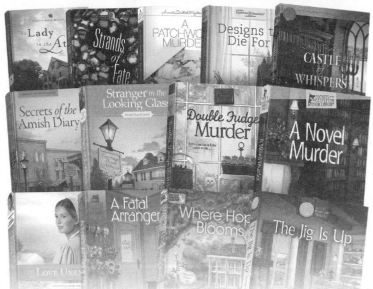